The Journey is
at times be
the life chang ○

[signature]

Connections:

A Journey of Love and

Autism

1

Connections:

A Journey of Love and Autism

Lynn A. Shebat, M.Ed.

1010 Publishing Company

ISBN English: 9781099356001

ISBN Spanish: 978-0-9993978-5-5

Printed in the United States of America.

Introduction

I was in Mrs. Patsy Mills' fourth-grade class. I was 10 years old, and the assignment was to present a book report with a presentation using large chart paper. My biggest fear as a child was to speak in front of my class and have drawings on this ambiguous chart paper. I didn't draw. So, I chose my book, the story of Helen Keller. I knew after reading it that, as a child myself, I could be that kind of helper-a teacher. It was fascinating, challenging, and totally inspiring to me. Years later, I found myself in college with a few more interests, majoring in Special Education. I had no idea what was in store for me in the next decades of my life, but I knew I had found my place in the universe.

2017-2018:

In the course of a year that I worked on writing this book, life has happened.

I lost my father. I lost a precious student, only five years old, a twin. I lost my beloved Josie, our sweet golden retriever, and a companion to my daughters. I was selected as Teacher of the Year. I have completed 30 years of teaching but still teach. My middle daughter graduated from Oxford. My youngest daughter turned 18 years old. I traveled to Italy for the first time with my husband. My oldest daughter told me that I would soon be a grandmother.

Life is good and beautiful. Be in the moment, present in your life and your child's life. Make it as magical as you can for your child, your family, and yourself.

Preface

Present day:

Every summer, I have the opportunity to spend some time at the beach with my mom and my sister. I grew up spending my summers there with my grandparents and great-grandparents. It is my happy place.

It is a quiet area with old Florida beaches and a picturesque lighthouse. In the little gift lighthouse shop, I bought a journal. It was a few summers ago, in June of 2017, that my urgency to write became defined. I thought I could write some thoughts and maybe someday gather it all together to put some understanding to my life. Raising a child with a disability (or just any children) gobbles up the minutes in a day until they are only memories, and you are busy with the next day.

I began to write in my journal. Looking at the cover with the word *believe* on it and a picture of a dragonfly, it spoke to me. I told myself to just start writing. I began, and I could not stop. My heart was pouring out, the story was to be written, and the time was now. On this porch, where my grandmother told us her stories and wrote her poems, here I sit and compose my story. The butterflies that reflect your light dance around the bushes that I played by as a child. What I know for sure is that love abounds. There is no start or finish between the generations where there is love. Life and death continue, as does the love for the family and friends that came into our lives and then left.

This is a story, a journey, and hopefully a compass, on how to help your child with a disability, or a classroom full of children with various disabilities, to develop to their fullest potential. This is my path, which I have walked professionally and personally. My desire is to share ideas, strategies, and hope that will enhance your own path with these beautiful children that are ours.

Dedications

To Brianna, thank you for letting me tell our story. You are my soul.

To Elana, my middle daughter, my little angel that sacrificed her time and her mom without a choice. You are a gift to your sister, to me, and to the world.

To Amanda, you, my first child, you taught me everything about being a mother. You taught your baby sister to speak and experience pure joy. You have always been her second momma. You are a blessing in every sense of the word.

To Leslie, thank you for the creative space to begin this labor of love.

To Mom, you have been along for the ride from the start. For the days you provided me respite and time to finish this project, I will be forever grateful. You always knew me, understood me, and loved me. I passed that on to my children. They will pass it on to theirs.

To my father, I miss you. You gave me the strength to make it through the hard days.

To Ellyn, you were by my side through thick and thin. I learned from the best.

To Diem, my heart is with you in Heaven. Beebop loves you.

To Sareon, you carry my heart on Earth. Dragonfly. To my friend who always believed this was possible. You told me "Writers write." You gave me direction. I'm grateful.

Table of Contents

Present day:

1

The Dreams and Nightmares

Graduation came with job offers and a chance to start my dream of working with children. Not just any kids, but the kind that needed understanding, special training, patience, and a teacher who would move Heaven and Earth to help them. I loved these little broken- winged birds. Angels who were dropped from Heaven to teach us mere mortals.

I began my career, if you can call it that, in the city that I grew up in, Miami, Florida. Hotter than a desert at times with an occasional ocean breeze if you were lucky. I took a job with a non-profit organization as a therapist for infants to children up to three years old. I was barely 21 myself, and although my intentions were great, I definitely was lacking in life experience. I innocently told each young mother how precious their baby was but didn't realize the depth of their pain. My intent was to show that I didn't see any obstacles for their little ones. We would work together and fix the things that needed repaired. I did not comprehend the torture they had endured sitting in hospitals for months, anticipating the outcomes of surgeries and the anguish of seizures, with the medications and numerous medical personnel predicting the future of their newborns.

A dream of a baby, a family, a new life dashed in a diagnosis of unforeseen hardship. Broken hearts, broken marriages, and broken families due to the unmistakable fear of the unknown—the Bermuda Triangle of what comes next. The health of the baby; the unmet developmental milestones; the medical expenses; and the waiting lists of therapies, appropriate schools, and doctors; to name only the beginning of what would change these families forever.

A thousand times, I would ask the universe to forgive me for my naivety.

Only at the birth of my own first daughter would I understand what only life can teach you. I would learn volumes in that sacred moment when you become a parent for the first time. The hopes, the dreams for yourself, and for your child that are seeded. The unquenchable desire to give them the world. To meet every need and shelter them with love. To watch them sleep like cherubs only to catch your breath at the sheer beauty of their innocence.

Learning and loving my field of study, Special Education, I began to develop my skills as a young teacher. I enhanced my bravery, my understanding, and my sense of humor over the next several years. At the same time, I was a mother of a precocious toddler with the hope of having another. I dreamt of a family, a house, a cat or dog, a fenced in backyard, a swing set, and security. The dream of so many: the planning, the preparation, an answered prayer, a life.

A few years later, with a kindergartner as my little companion going with me to work in a new school, life was moving. I was the teacher of first-grade through third-grade students with various exceptionalities, mainly behavior disorders with a few kids on the spectrum on my caseload. I was loving my life, my job, my child. Everything was falling into place and life was good.

Soon after, I began to feel the familiar nausea that a developing baby creates in your body. I would be blessed twice. My happiness could not have been more of an extension to the love I already had for my little girl. She would have a sibling, never to be alone, and all my dreams were coming true. My passion for my job continued. I had a purpose. I had the skills to reach every child. I made a difference. I could fix the broken. I could love the unloved. I promised to always be their advocate. In a way, I was saving both of us. What I was doing mattered. That brought me so much satisfaction. Then came that day that changed me. The lines between professional and personal were blurred.

I was deep in therapy with this one particular little guy. A precious, however, angry young soul who had been out of control for most of the morning. After utilizing several strategies to diffuse his aggression, he was put into the time-out room, which was the therapy procedure at that time. Once in the room, he scaled the walls like Spiderman for several minutes. I spoke with him constantly through the monitor and did my best to calm him down while taking the danger away from the other students. At the point that I was sure I could control him, I opened the door. I calmly told him, "It's okay, I'm here, let's sit down and talk. He came down off the wall, plunging his foot with force into my newly pregnant belly. The wind knocked out of me, I tried to calm down, and saying to myself, "I'm okay, it's all fine." I continue my job. My student is well. All my students are fine. I did my job. "I'll be alright," I prayed.

I was experiencing some minor spotting, which freaked me out, so I went to the doctor's office the next day. I was due for a regular prenatal checkup anyway, so I went in early with the whole family. My daughter at five years old, in tow, would learn about her new sibling. It was a happy day, except that I didn't feel right and continued to pray. The technician entered with the ultrasound wand and spoke to me, but I didn't hear her words. She left the room, telling us that she'll be right back. "I can't interpret these results, she stated, telling us she will go get the doctor.

I grew up in a medical home with a father who was a doctor. I knew the signs, the distance, the mannerly approach, the code words. The doctor came in and listened to my belly, and with what seemed like a shout, stated in front of my precious daughter, only a baby herself, that there was no heartbeat! The baby was dead. I stopped breathing.

"What did he just say?" I looked at my child, trying desperately to say, "It is okay, mommy's here." That wasn't true. Her father took her out of the room and I screamed, saying I don't understand. "Call my father!" I insisted. This isn't right. I feel this baby. My breasts hurt, my belly has butterflies. My baby is still in me. The doctor got my dad on the phone, who in perfect medical vocabulary gave me the statistics for miscarriage. I told him "I am not miscarrying; the baby is here." He said, "I am sorry, honey." My heart was broken, still is, and will always be.

I imagine a depression set in for a while. I tried to breathe. I tried to let go of the saddest moment of my life. I had a beautiful little girl that needed her mommy back. I had to come back for her. I also had to go back to a job that was so much of my life, and I couldn't be scared, angry, or bitter, yet I was all of that.

It is strange how when you go through life experiences, painful experiences, you come out differently. Perhaps you develop strength that you didn't have before, but you are also changed forever. There are parts of you that will never be recovered. There will also be powers that come from within that you would never believe you had. A fire, a strength to be used for when you need it the most, will arise. Instincts are honed on a level that you will see what you need to see ahead of time. Life will not send you many more curveballs that you won't be able to catch or at least not be hit with directly. You grow with the good and the bad, and the unforeseen. Maybe you grow to help yourself in the future or to help others. However, it's for certain we move forward, for that is our only choice.

I did return to the classroom. I drew my lines carefully. I never got hurt again—not like that kind of hurt. My defenses were up. I asked for help when I needed it. I took breaks when needed. I followed my instincts. I listened better to my surroundings. I forgave. I forgave myself for lapses in judgment, for not foreseeing the danger, for not being perfect. I probably became more focused on my career following that tragedy. I knew that there were babies needing help. I knew it took instincts, special eyes and ears, and a heart for the long days.

The student I had in my classroom, suffering from the crack addiction passed on at birth by his mother; the family of children with special needs living in sheer poverty; the child from another country institutionalized because of a minor disability and the years it would take to pull him out of the damage it caused; those students were mine to mend. Together with those students and many more who crossed my path, we started traveling on a road of therapy and fun to find our way. I had the strength and the passion, and I was developing my skills with every student.

After about four years, my second miracle happened. My second child was born. She was an amazing and long-awaited gift. Elana was born with jet black hair, which fell out sooner than I expected, only to be replaced by the whitest hair on her little angelic head.

A little brown-eyed blonde, after a dark brunette, she added to the variety of our family. I had my two children. Two sisters to share a friendship for all their days. My dream was back on track. Life was good. I took to motherhood of an infant like a fish to water. I was calm and relaxed. I was blessed beyond words. She was a bit cranky, and always hungry, but I relished every second of this opportunity again to watch this tiny life develop.

I went to work part-time, enjoying a job share opportunity with a colleague, also a new mother. Perfect in every way, it was a new start, a chance to breathe fully once again. I share these very personal moments to show you that I am human. I lived a life with multiple experiences, both in my classroom and in my home. I learned from those experiences to help me understand the child with autism and all disabilities to some extent. I took these lessons and became a better teacher and parent.

"In order to write about life first you must live it." Ernest Hemingway

2

The Beginning

Brianna was a surprise! She was a sweet and wonderful surprise to add to our family. I had always wanted a big family. My pregnancies with my two other girls were fine with only the usual precautions. While nursing Elana, my second, I found myself nauseous. I thought maybe I was getting sick. Instead, I found myself with child. I welcomed this little package with all my heart. I was tired, but I was overjoyed with the growth of my family.

My pregnancy with her at 36 was stressful. Ultrasounds, an amniocentesis, and all the other procedures were implemented. At three months, the ultrasound showed blood flow problems to the heart, which could've been indications of heart problems in the left ventricle.

Google was new at that time, and the search engines

were on fire on my computer as I self-diagnosed, looking for any and all possibilities. It freaked me out, to say the least, causing an emotional term of pregnancy. I tried to stay stress-free, but it was impossible. I prayed constantly. The next ultrasound took place, and I waited to hear the results. I wondered if it would it be a future of open-heart surgery on my infant? I had prayed with all my heart to make this not be the case. I wasn't strong enough of a mother for that. I was not that brave.

I prayed for her to be whole in every part of her body. She was tiny and innocent. Take me, I prayed, but please don't make her suffer and go through such torture as an infant. I was so frightened about what would be in store for us.

We walked around the mall at Christmastime, trying to kill time, in anticipation of the outcome. The nurse called and said these words, "The heart is perfectly developed. The ventricles are all there in the shape of a cross." Prayers answered. "Thank you, God!" I prayed in gratitude. I was going to dodge a bullet that I knew I could not bear. She was healthy in her heart, and my prayers were answered. We were going to be fine. My dream was back on track once again. Life was good, again. Once more, we would be blessed. Once more, we'd be safe from all the sadness that other parents would suffer through, as I walked next to them but not in their shoes.

We had to just wait for the birth of child number three, for this would be the last baby I would have. There was utter contentment in my heart. I had my beautiful family. We would be complete. We would be happy. My girls would have each other. They would have a friend in each other.

A letter to Bri:

To my littlest,

You are growing. You are sweet and smiley. You are my heart. You are rambling on with gibberish, but you are not talking. Your sisters spoke in sentences and paragraphs at your age. You are just the baby, take your time, my love.

Mommy

I had hoped it was a speech delay based on your sibling position. You were the baby after all and the youngest of three. Your siblings were speaking for you. According to the family stories, I used to do that for my little sister. It will come, I told myself.

Brianna looked right into my eyes. I wasn't worried, yet. I waited.   I waited for 13 months exactly. Her first birthday passed, and she was still nursing, growing, happy, and healthy. These were her first words at 13 months: mommy, ball, Elmo, and no! "That's okay," I told myself. It will come. My heart fluttered a little. My instincts were strong. I defensively pushed them away. I decided it was time. My heart did not settle down. My fears did not go away.

They became more intrusive. I was a veteran special education teacher. I knew the signs. I could ignore them no longer. I didn't want to see these signs. To me, she was perfect, in every way.

She was delayed in speech and climbed on everything. I had seen so much worse in my career. I told her it will be okay, and I told my heart the same.

I made the appointments, the evaluations, and the apologies for wasting everyone's time because I was a professional in this field.   I made friends with the pediatricians, the occupational therapists, and the speech therapists. I pretended to be working. These were my colleagues. I knew the drill. This was just something I would have to go through, then the professionals would tell me she was fine. I would speak this mantra that Bri is just waiting for us to hear her voice. She's her own spirit. She will speak when she is ready.

In the meantime, I would see what the experts had to say. They told me, "PDD-NOS, Pervasive Developmental Disorder, non- otherwise specified, not Autism, not Spectrum Disorder, not yet anyway." Basically, in my mind a diagnosis that meant they didn't know what it was. "The experts are wrong," I screamed to myself. "That's what they say when they don't really know," I repeated in anger. My frustration screamed, "Not my child, not Bri." "Not me," I whispered, selfishly.

It just didn't make sense. I couldn't process it. First of all, in a conversation with a higher being, I bargained, "Remember God, I wanted this career since I was a girl! Don't I get points for that," I questioned. I had dedicated my life up to that point to other children with disabilities and to their families. Seventeen years of heart and soul I'd given to that field. I loved my career. I was a natural, I argued. People even called me the "Autism Whisperer" at times, on my job. This is my life. My family and career are separate. Acceptance does not come.

Family members brought their opinions. Everyone had an opinion about my precious girl. Everyone was wrong, according to my heart at that time. I told myself that I will fix this. Mommy would come to the rescue. "I've got this," I claimed. I talked myself in and out of many arguments until I came up with an action plan. Bri began months of therapy at Children's Healthcare of Atlanta, the best of the best in pediatric care. I knew she was in good hands. I put our names on the list for the best developmental pediatrician in the country, Dr. Leslie Rubin, who happened to practice in Atlanta. I then proceeded to research. I read, watched, and studied everything that I could get my hands on. I researched genetics, immunizations, an autism diet, mercury in the environment, sensory diets, hyperbaric chambers, charcoal baths, minerals, chelation, and any other therapy on the books at that time. I taught myself everything I needed to know to be her best mother, therapist, and advocate. Game on, I rallied. I would learn to kick butt to autism.

Letter to Bri:

To Brianna,

You are adorable. Your eyes are still hazel colored. I wonder if you will have my eyes? You love your sisters. You play with dolls. You bring an entire gallon of milk up the stairs with your bottle and nipple in hand. That's probably not typical, but you make us laugh with your tenacity.

Adoringly, Mommy

3

The Time for Action

While reading the books, studying the research, and
getting basic training in ABA, Discrete Trial Therapy,
Bri and I began the work. Our setting was her
highchair. The materials were a ball, an Elmo doll, a
block, and pictures on the table. I presented the
materials in a discrete trial format to my little baby
with purpose. One item at a time, I introduced the
object, the vocabulary, and the reinforcement. I used
Cheerios with her because it was always a favorite with
all of my girls.

I held up the ball. "Bri," I said softly, "Touch the ball,
say ball." Next, I presented two items at a time, a block
and a ball, and then said again, "Touch the ball." My
heart begged her to make the right choice. I just
wanted her to show me that she understood. I pleaded
with her to do it for mommy! I urged her to just show
me what I already knew—that she was in there. She

was trapped in the silence of autism. I sang to her and told her I was right there with her. "I won't leave you," I promised her. "I will be your voice. We will make this happen." My heart pleaded with her to touch the ball, say ball, to speak. Day after day, we would repeat the same practices. I would change up the items with the same concepts. I would use a different ball or Elmo, but I would consistently say words to reach her to engage with our therapy. I would label the item and hold it at an equal distance, prodding her to touch the ball. The strategy was for her to demonstrate awareness of the connection between the word and the object.

Her receptive language was evident with her comprehension of things said to her in the home environment, but she needed to demonstrate that understanding in these small increments. I knew she knew what a ball was and Elmo. Those items were her whole world except for food. The trick was in getting her to identify them through the language.

Verbal behavior, the expression of the label, was the

golden nugget. Before that skill was the receptive demonstration of reaching out to touch the item on demand. It was tedious work, but it paid off after many months of intensive work. She finally gave approximations of the word, "ball", with the beginning sound followed by the "aa" sound. It was progress. It was what we had been working on for so long, but it was only a crack in the window. We would have to carry on, week after month after years to expand her vocabulary, begging for those elicit words and receptive understanding.

The therapy of ABA and Discrete Trial is very helpful with the majority of children who have various language and skill deficits. It is taught with the smallest of demands to assist in gaining the independence from the child through the use of prompts. For verbal behavior, I would give Bri the Elmo at a distance, teaching her to ask for the toy with her vocal approximations, or better yet, saying the name, "Elmo". Then once she tried to say it, I would give it to her, and say," Yes, that's Elmo," reinforcing with positive praise and an occasional Cheerio, although with Bri, Elmo was always enough. As we progressed with the therapy, I introduced the ball, as well as Elmo, thus encouraging her to discriminate between the two.

Through these daily lessons several times a day, she heard the language that we so desired to hear from her. Each object that we added would add to her vocabulary. I started slowly, and didn't add too much to the therapy session until she was really mastering the concept. I talked to her constantly and invoked every family member around to also talk with her consistently, by conversation or song, labeling everything in her environment. Through these experiences and those of the many children that I have taught through the years, I believe that language bombardment in a simple format will assist with language development. They have to hear it, see it, and then we have to check to see that they understand it.

Do your own research with ABA Discrete Trial through a board-certified behavior analyst (BCBA) that you may find beneficial to be a part of your team. There are many different therapies that benefit children at different stages, and you have to see what works best for your family. I found this therapy to be a good way to start a baseline for Brianna, which was her four known words, and then went from there. I also mentioned that I did this from the highchair because otherwise I couldn't contain her or gain her attention. The benefit of teaching in small increments is the goal—it is simple or discrete. If I wanted her to look at me, to give me eye contact, I would say, "Look at Mommy!" All I needed was a second glance, and she was running all over the place. I would pick her up, and say "Look at Mommy, look at Mommy." Practice makes perfect, or technically, reinforcing the behavior gets the behavior after much guidance and practice.   I felt like my daughter was locked in the darkness of autism, and   I wasn't going to allow that. Our work continued. Therapy also continued. I had to glance over at my other children, on this journey with us but not asked if they wanted to join. No choices were given; we had to move forward.

I wouldn't stop until Bri was talking and less frustrated. I would not stop until Bri was with us totally and completely. My others were babies, as well. They needed me, too. I was so tired, but I was driven. If I had stopped to take inventory of my surroundings at that time with my children, my career, my marriage, my home; if I had taken a breath, progress would have stopped in my mind. I was in the beginning stages of becoming a Warrior Mom. I had lost some battles, but I refused to lose my daughter.

"A journey is a person in itself: not two are alike. And all plans, safeguards, policing, and coercion are fruitless. We find that after years of struggle that we do not take a trip: a trip takes us." John Steinbeck

4

The Early Years

Denial is a term often used when describing parents who are not quite ready to investigate a disability. That moment we hang on to when we know our child and think that we can handle the current situation. For me, working in a psychoeducational center for children with varying disabilities, especially autism, made it very difficult. I was surrounded by professionals who could hear the pain in my inquiries about Brianna's development. My own assistant, my friend, could see what I wasn't ready to.

I remember a night when we were all out eating sushi, and Bri was just staring at a glass frame holding a shiny red kimono. She was about two years old, and I was so angry at my friends' interpretations of her behavior. I defended it profusely, claiming that all babies do that, knowing full well there was a problem. Another time, I left the kids with my sister while my husband and I went on a trip. When I came home, my sister would point out the flapping that Bri would do. Again, I defend her behavior and made excuses to explain away her behavior. I wasn't ready to accept that anything was different with my daughter. I had already started receiving evaluation results from speech and occupational therapists. I felt like I was doing something to help with her communication deficits. I thought it would be a quick fix with a few sessions of therapy. Being in the field of special education didn't make it any easier for me than any other parent. I knew the signs. I could diagnose someone else's child in a heartbeat. When you are in the parent's seat, no matter what your education is, it is never easy to see the truth. I was not different, maybe even worse.

To this day, I still see so much more potential in Bri than others do. That is the natural position of being a parent. Like me, when you are ready to see what you want to dismiss, you will open up your path and proceed to the most beneficial road for your child.

We had a diagnosis. We had therapies in place. We had a beautiful baby girl that had a few idiosyncrasies. She had super strength, was extremely active, and was still not saying five words. Time was passing. They say that Einstein did not speak until he was five years old. There are several important intelligent people that didn'tspeak until they were ready. I held out for this hope for as long as I could.

One thing for sure was that Bri was understanding language. Several languages, in fact, elicited a correct behavior from her. Her grandmother spoke French, Hebrew, and Arabic around her, and she asked from Bri things like "Bring Grandma her shoes.", or "Turn off the light.", and Bri would follow through with the direction. She understood all that was being said. She just wouldn't talk back except for words that sounded like gibberish. She babbled away and talked to everyone, just not in any intelligible language.

Life was moving fast and forward. I was still teaching. The girls were growing up. I had to go back to work full time, and that meant putting both my younger girls in daycare. I chose the best and closest one to my work. I had just landed a new job close to home in a good school that housed a psycho-educational center. I was so excited to be so close to home, but my heart was a little achy with the guilt of leaving my babies again. I convinced myself that a baby program would be the best for Bri and her sister. My middle daughter was almost four years old then, and she was excited to be going to a big girl school. I was confident that Bri would learn to talk by being around her same- age peer group. The reality of what happened was that Bri learned how to unlock all the adult locks on the childproof doors, flush all the baby toilets, turn on all the faucets, and become the greatest escape artist since Houdini.

I was puzzled at this behavior, and like all protective parents assumed it must be due to lack of supervision on the part of the school. It didn't even dawn on me that these behaviors were part of an interesting development with my child. Months later, the director called me in and told me that maybe this wasn't the best place for my child. Those were fighting words for this mother tiger! I couldn't believe the arrogance, the incompetence, or the cruelty of telling me this. Bri wasn't even two years old! I was furious.

I thought about quitting my job. That would have been financial heartache, as well as a personal one. I had managed both my career and family, if you can call it management, up until that point. I was angry, confused, and protective of the most innocent of babies. I started looking for different programs, which added to my frustration of ruining my perfectly planned life. I wanted it all, and I was going to keep trying until I figured out this path for us. I chose a Montessori school, which would be a great help. An educational approach geared toward the internally motivated child would provide the solution, I was looking for. After all, in my mind, there was nothing wrong with my misunderstood toddler. In fact, I soothed myself with the ideas of how Brianna was too advanced for the regular toddler school, and that's why she was demonstrating these behaviors. The thought of an open space filled with toys, puzzles, and math and science centers would be the world at her hands. I hoped with my entire being that she would go into this beautiful environment and show everyone how incredibly intelligent she was. I hoped that with this much motivation and free space, she would speak. That's all I wanted. At this point, I just wanted her to be happy, safe, and protected from judgment, and rating scales to tell me how imperfect she was in her current placement.

It is a cruel and not necessary reality check that we as young parents get hit with. It comes from caring people sometimes. Teachers, doctors, and therapist mean well, but with most cases we are not ready for any cold truths. We hold in our heart a child, our baby, and all of the dreams of the future, and then we are told to slow down and take a second look. It's best if we are the first people in our children's lives to notice the delays, but at the same time, our hearts are so full of love that we cannot yet see what others may. It's this time in my memory, and for my families that have felt the same, I ask you only to catch your breath, to love the moment you're in with your child, and listen to the helpers, if that is what they are, with a grain of salt. It doesn't really change your world, but it just slows it down for the time that you need.

So, we started the Montessori school. Bri loved the environment. There was a lot of stimuli—toys, housekeeping centers, and baby dolls were in every corner, and of course, other babies. She was happy exploring her new school and seemed to be adjusting just fine.

Along came Ms. Dianne, the teacher of the two-year-old's' room. She was the sweetest, strongest, most instinctive human being that I have ever met. She *knew* toddlers! She had a wealth of experience. She was a power in her own right, and the way she managed that classroom was nothing short of magnificent. Bri was her muse, and Ms. Dianne was hers. I know Ms. Dianne was an angel for me. At a time of desperation, she gave me hope. She was also instrumental in teaching me parenting skills with

Brianna. She taught me about the structure of her classroom—how the children would put their little things away independently. This little band of babies would sit on the circle carpet and wait for her instruction. I had never heard a two-year-old use the words "not acceptable" before seeing her class. It was hilarious but effective. She insisted that Bri would only carry one Elmo while going down the slide and not five! I never thought of it, maybe not even noticed it, but it was a constraint for Bri to play with all of her toys simultaneously. I just wanted her to have what made her happy. I didn't understand at the time that our children tend to hoard their possessions as if they will lose them forever if they put them down. Ms. Dianne was there to show me things I was not ready to see. She taught me, and Bri, in a firm but loving manner that made all the difference. Ms. Dianne insisted on circle time with full participation, following directions, and most importantly nap time. Trust me, that was a novelty for both of us. Bri had never napped. Another concept that I didn't grasp at that time in my life was the presence of sleeping abnormalities or irregularities.

Bri wouldn't nap, but she wouldn't sleep early either.
She would just stop when she had no more batteries
charged. She would rest just enough, and then come
back to being fully awake and ready to go again. It's a
pattern of behavior of our children on the spectrum,
and sometimes other disabilities, that I was not aware
of. Somehow, it didn't come up in graduate school at
the time.

I learned so much from living it, day and night. Ms.
Dianne treated Bri like everyone else in the class. She
was a gift from heaven for me. We were starting to see
progress from the beginning. Bri was responding to
the structure. She hugged all of her baby friends and
waved goodbye at the end of the day. She did try to
steal their toys, and especially a forgotten pacifier, but
we were seeing improvements.

The main reason I write about Ms. Dianne is that as the
saying goes, "It takes a village." I cannot tell you how
true that is. As an admitted control freak when it

comes to my kids and especially Bri, I had to teach myself to let go at times and ask for help. These two things do not come naturally to me. So early on, learn to seek out the helpers, and let them help. I am still trying to this day, and Bri is now 18. Resources are getting to be a little more available but are still costly. It's also necessary to find the time to build relationships with the caretakers for our children. If they cannot speak or tell us that they are safe, it's up to us to ensure they are. That is why I am still looking for the right help. Often, a college student who is in the field may be promising choice. Unfortunately, they often go back to school or start their real jobs eventually. The best practice is to find the same- age peer while your child is young.

If you're lucky enough to find a motivated peer or friend for your child who could grow up with them, that would be ideal. You never know the positive influence that would provide for both your child and the peer helper. After all, that's how I fell into a career that I love and have always had a passion for. Maybe you can encourage the next generation of special education teachers, therapists, or even doctors? In the world we were thrust into, we don't have a lot of personal choices. If we think outside of the box and work on building a community together to support our children, everyone benefits.

Montessori was a great transition from the traditional daycare setting for us. However, it was not enough. After many hours of thought and watching Bri in the circle of other typically developing babies, I realized that I would have to seek out more support. I began the evaluation process for services through the public-school system that I worked for. At this time, I was teaching middle school children with severe autism and behavioral difficulties. The idea that my own baby would be like the children I was teaching was painful. I couldn't bear to look into a crystal ball that would show her suffering from a lack of independence, behavioral deficits, and language disorders. Yes, I felt like a hypocrite, but at that time she seemed so far away from that age group, and she was my toddler.

Remember, it's a process to leave behind the denial of anything wrong and to also take the step towards acceptance.

Following an evaluation, she was eligible for a placement in a part- time special needs' preschool. The program was housed at the school right next to mine. She would have to take a little bus from the preschool back to her Montessori program. A school bus for a two-year-old to go across the street—this thought almost shut me down. My baby girl on a bus was more like a nightmare for me than an offer of help. I didn't have any other way since I was working.   I couldn't really leave my class in the middle of the day. So, I reluctantly accepted to start this new program.

Bri loved the baby kitchen, but she was obsessed and wouldn't leave it, thus the ensuing multiple tantrums. It wasn't long before I began to get the sad faces on her communication report about her behavior. "Killing me slowly," I used to curse. In hindsight, I think I would have just stopped my world and taught her myself. I have guilted myself into that thought a million times over. I learned though that she needed those other babies, and most definitely needed those teachers and therapist to be her model, and not her mom. I settled with teaching her every other second of her day, as the village model was what we needed. I found out that she loved art therapy at two-years-old with Ms. Wendy. When coaxed away from the beloved kitchen set, she would smile and giggle at the modeling clay, paint, and shaving cream. At that time, the only way I would've known this was a simple polaroid that showed a big beautiful smile on the face my angel. The face that I was convinced would've had been crying for me all day. It was nice to learn that wasn't true. To this day, as I am mentoring young teachers, the first piece of advice I give is to photograph everything possible, especially our children who cannot go home and tell us about their day. It provided me not only with information about her day, but it also provided me with comfort.

This time was the personal introduction to art therapy, music therapy, occupational therapy, and speech therapy in the school system at the early intervention stage. As a teacher, those times were often an opportunity for me to catch up on paperwork. As a parent, it was nothing short of a miracle, to watch the therapist bring something out in Bri. The therapists were exactly what Bri needed to open up her world. The most important things I learned from these early years of intervention was that Bri would perform differently for different people. That was an important lesson for me to understand the consistency and generalization of skills. Bri would listen and pick and choose who she wanted to follow through with directions. It was usually dependent upon who had the better reinforcement. They would show me, the mom—the special education teacher— the skills that she was developing in that environment. That was shocking to me.

One day when I was doing our home therapy, back in the high chair, I showed her a cookie. I showed her the sign language prompt for a cookie. She looked at me and broke into song— The "C is for cookie" song from Sesame Street. I almost fainted! She was learning to sing. She was learning the words to several songs and articulating her vocabulary perfectly, even though she wouldn't label a cookie for anything in the world. Stubborn little soul!

"I want all my senses engaged. Let me absorb the world's variety and uniqueness." Maya Angelou

5

Starting from Here—Again

We had a new starting point. A new baseline with emerging skills that seemed to develop overnight. She was always surprising me with her new tricks. The beauty of that was in the understanding of her obvious awareness. She was paying attention, even if she didn't appear to be. So, we sang. We would sing, "C is for Cookie", and then we would stop. I would hold up the cookie. Asking her, "What do you want?" I asked her to say "cookie." I then would wait, show her the sign, and wait. What seemed like a thousand repetitions, probably was about 10 per session. She then would put her precious little hands together and show me the sign for cookie. She didn't say it yet, but she performed on demand. My heart sang. We continued to sing. We sang everything—the "ABC" song, "Count to Five" songs, the "Veggie" song. Her favorites, like "If You're Happy and You Know It"—we sang all of them and she responded. The lesson learned at that juncture was that she was listening. She was taking it all in   at rapid speed, and she was giving it back in song. In a beautiful, rhythmic, angelic, although very low tone, she was communicating. As my father used to say, "Contact!" We had made contact. We were connecting on her platform. It became my greatest task to figure out how to do more of the same.

I made up songs about going to sleep, brushing our teeth, and going potty. The funny thing is my other girls who are now women, still sing the potty song. I sang to her every song I knew. I sang the classics: the Beatles, Simon and Garfunkel, Elton John, Billy Joel, even a little Frank Sinatra in honor of my father. I played Mozart, Beethoven, and Itzhak Perlman. I went to the library and checked out Jazzy Classic for Kids, selections from Motown, and songs from around the globe. Drum beats and violin, piano and flute, chants and poetry. I gave her whatever I could get my hands on. This was before streaming music. It's easier now to have the variety at your disposal. I even made CDs to play in the car.

She showed me with her behavior which songs she didn't like, and then made it known what she wanted to be played over and over again. Sometimes, to increase her tolerance, I played the less preferred for just a minute longer. I then used the opportunity to get the language from her to approximate a request.

Our world of music and communication grew and generalized to all environments and all members of the family. She listened and responded more consistently to the song, and it became our language of choice. Later, when I explored the true science of music therapy, I learned about the power behind the beat for our babies on the spectrum. To make her language more functional, I had to get back to the basics, eventually. While keeping the songs going, I used them for reinforcement. If you are new to the world of autism and all the vocabulary, this will become your new common language. Basically, every task you teach must be followed up with reinforcement. In other words, these special angels usually don't perform for the sake of pleasing others. That part of their brain functions differently, so they basically work for what they want, or if you happen to have a trick up your sleeve, for the reinforcement. They will work for the reinforcement. Later, they'll perform the same task in a routine with less or no reinforcement, but that takes time.

The structure or patterns our children desire are comforting to them. Once they have the skill mastered, they will perform skills independently, within the structure (for example, hanging up their book bag in the classroom or putting their shoes in the same place at home.) In the beginning, a teacher or parent may reinforce this behavior for months, and then all of the sudden the child will perform it independently. This happens when the child takes ownership of the task, is independent at the full task, and basically is self-motivated to complete it. A quick note about reinforcement: As a parent, you know what your child likes and what they are willing to work for, or are at least interested in. Although those interests change sometimes quite often, sometimes they stay the same. Bri loved Elmo from her babyhood until present. The funny thing was that for Bri, she had backup loves. She also loved Dora and Winnie the Pooh. It was wonderful for Bri to have so many things that brought her happiness. It never occurred to me that it could be a problem. One day when Bri was about four-years-old, a very proficient therapist was working with her during an ABA session, and she would not discriminate for the favored reinforcement. Meaning, when the task was presented to Bri she didn't do it, it wasn't reinforced, because if she couldn't have Elmo, she would just go and get Dora. This was a problem for her therapy sessions because I knew she could master the discrete task like touch the ball, but she just giggled and got down and ran around. A session like that will teach a good therapist to tighten the reigns on both the child and the reinforcements. For my precocious daughter, the game of chase turned out to be much more reinforcing.

Now at that time, I was not perceptive enough to know

the difference in her behavioral responses. The therapist told me to get together a basket of all of her favorite toys. I did it. I knew she loved those items. That was a start. With Bri and all children, their interests do change from time to time. It's tricky to find the exact reinforcement to entice them to perform a task. In the classroom, it's even more difficult to find the currency of so many of your students. At the beginning of every year during pre-planning, I send home a reinforcement inventory to the parents. It usually covers favorite items in all categories from food, toys, television shows, sensory needs, activities, and more. There are many ideas for templates for reinforcement inventories online. A child's interests are never constant; therefore, we must listen and watch carefully to learn their new interests to keep the therapy in motion, and the learning continuing.

We used music. I still use music to transition, to reinforce, to calm, and to dance. With music, we celebrate and communicate. With any tool, I find it best to broaden the interest as much as possible. Like with music, vary the tone, the volume, the rhythm, the speed, and the beat for the songs to keep them interesting to the child. I find this philosophy works with everything: toys, food, places, people, tasks, and activities, to name a few. The more they are exposed to all their interests, as well as their protests, the maximum the benefit. The mere nature of autism is to auto or isolate interests, space, and language, as well as everything else in their world. It is self-limiting. The smaller the box they create for themselves, the safer it feels at the time.

Our job as parents, therapists, and teachers is to broaden their worlds in every area so that the world is bigger, while remaining safe to them and not increasing their anxiety. Anxiety is such a common word these days, and everybody seems to be anxious. For our children with communication disorders and sensory regulations deficits, it is important to manage anxiety on a daily basis. The fear of the unknown for our kids, and the anxiety that it can produce, limit our children in attempting new tasks or eating new food, or even eating at all. It must be addressed systematically. Understanding our children's behavior through play, meltdowns, or hesitation to try new things takes time. Even going into a room or tolerating a sound will take time. Just when I thought I understood one area that I had worked on with Bri, another would present itself. This happens in behavior consistently. You can expect that when you address an area of deficit or a behavior, that behavior will increase before it decreases. This is the science of behavior. Knowing and expecting the behavioral increases will also help you in identifying the next step for your child. With my daughter, I struggled the most with her being so innocent, so small, and so frustrated without language. This, in turn, added to my frustration and my fear. I questioned everything I knew about the behavioral sciences and   all the strategies I had used for years with other children who were my students. I knew that when I was trying to get this little bitty stubborn girl to say a word to label an object and she would throw herself down in frustration, that I had to be stronger. I had to hold out for that word and repeat it until I got it from her. I was painfully aware that her screaming would increase before I got that word. I had to continue, and so will you. The facts are difficult sometimes, and the work is exhausting, but when it's your child looking at you with big eyes and you are their interpreter, their voice, and their parent, you do the work. It is like looking into the darkest abyss and knowing you have no choice but to dive in and save your child.

"You must do the things you think you cannot do." Eleanor Roosevelt

6

The Therapy

The years following became a whirlwind of therapies, schedule changes, doctor appointments, books read, and conferences attended. Obsessive purchasing of therapy items, toys, Elmo's, puzzles, and software, without slowing down. I found myself for the next decade, searching for the unattainable. I wanted the secret to unlocking the puzzle that we call autism.

Brianna was so precious. She was beautiful with the thickest waves of brunette hair, and hazel eyes with the flicker of sunshine sparkling within. She had no aggression, rare tantrums or meltdowns, and was just perfect in my eyes. I'm confident that my helicopter parenting was obvious to everyone but myself. My biggest fear at that time was that she would get stuck in a developmental stage and not progress. At the same time, it was so easy to hold her and kiss her and tell her how much I loved her. If only love were enough, but it was not, so we had work to do. The work had to continue with every morning, every attempt at language, every car ride, every occasion that somehow seemed different to her. Initially, the framework of her therapy centered around speech and occupational therapy. Both therapies independently and together created a pathway to independence for the next level. I took her to the appointments after I had been teaching all day. I watched the clock, put my middle school students on the bus, grabbed my belongings, and then picked up my own two children from elementary and preschool, then raced to her therapy.

In the parking lot, Bri would protest. She would cling to me with a death grip upon entering the building. My other baby girl would be fussy, hungry, and ready to go home. She wasn't ready to watch her sister "play", while she sat in the observation room with Mommy. These are the sacrifices we make as parents of multiple children when one needs more of us than planned. Everyone pitches in, everyone suffers, and everyone benefits—it's a vicious cycle at times. I promised them both ice cream, a trip to the park, or anything else they wanted, but first we had to attend therapy. I remember watching the young therapist work with my tired little bunny, and Bri would refuse to perform to her true potential. I wanted to tap on the window of the observation room and say, "Do it this way, try this." As a professional first, it was so difficult to let someone else be in charge. It seemed like it was a waste of time. As her mother, I knew how to bring the best out of Bri. It was a difficult time of acceptance. I had to learn to allow other people to work with Bri. It was a long while before I appreciated the process. Then, they started pulling out the magic from within. Bri laughed at the sight of a new dollhouse with tiny people and baby furniture. The work began to evolve. She jumped up and down, sometimes pointing and sometimes babbling. The therapist patiently asked, "What do you want?" I cringed as Bri struggled to demonstrate any type of expressive language. I felt her pain. I felt the wait time as if it were hours.

Then it started: "House," she said. "House, house,

house!" By the time the house was in front of her, she had said it five times. The tears came streaming down my face behind the window. Elana, my middle daughter who was sitting next to me asked me," Why is mommy crying?" I replied, "I'm happy, baby, Mommy is very happy."

The steps involved in the beginning are treacherous. The promise I can make to you is that it is worth the work. The early intervention— the earlier the better, the more intense the better—is shown to be effective time after time. I have seen it so many times with my students who have crossed my path, and especially with my own daughter. Remember the point I made earlier about the village? It remains constant throughout your journey with your child. Your friends, your family, and your team who you work to put into place to support you and your child is the most important base you can provide for all. You can't do this alone. I tried. I tried to mastermind her whole therapy life as well as her daily life. I found myself exhausted and losing hope at times. Running on a crazy treadmill of work, home, family, therapy, children, sports, and school events, with a traveling husband while the kids were young left me to do it all. I mentally couldn't even think. All I could do was pack up kids, take them places, do the work, and repeat. My family wasn't in the same town. One of the biggest mistakes I made early on was not trusting anyone to help or even watch Bri for a little while. My fear of having a child who could not voice when things may not be right or even unpleasant for her, created an unreasonable obsession of mine, that I could never leave her with anyone except family. Truthfully, I still struggle with this due to changing people in her life. Finding constant support is difficult. My family is available on occasion.   I find that it benefits the child so much when they do have other caregivers besides the parent. The child tends to get locked into the relationship with a few special people and not really generalize those relationships with others. It is good to branch out, and in a safe environment, allow yourself and your child to experience different people. Everything about autism is not in learning new tasks or concepts, but in generalizing what they learned to the bigger picture. It's what allows the child to develop and to be able to participate in the world in a more typical fashion.

Bri's speech and occupational therapy continued, and then the battle with the health insurance companies became an issue. New to this side of the table, I quickly learned that I was going to have to battle for my daughter's therapy needs. I had the best insurance that a teacher can have. The plan covered 9 sessions with each therapy or 18 sessions with one field. How was I supposed to make that decision? It was ridiculous. She was three years old, and just starting to make progress. So, I did what any mother would do. I fought. I wrote appeals. I spoke to office managers and learned the system the best that I could. I didn't beat the system, but I understood what I was up against. With logistics presented, I worked around the system. I chose by default to co-treat. I joined my sessions with occupational therapy and speech, keeping my hour therapy but splitting my service time. Bri had two therapists working with her at the same time. Joining their superpowers, it was a good plan for my daughter.

The occupational therapist placed her on a platform swing, a small flat board swing above the mat about a foot, and she swung her. She positioned Bri's tiny hands on the rope and told her to sit still. This was no small feat for my little action baby.

While Bri swung, the speech therapist showed her a sign and verbalized her requested word, "more", and then suddenly stopped the swing. Bri puzzled, fussed, and showed her discontent. The speech therapist then repeated the process. Sign, word, sign, then push the swing, and stop the swing. After several attempts and stopping and keeping the swing still, Bri finally placed her long little fingers together to sign for more. I won't tell you that I cried, that's a given!

It's a very emotional and tedious journey at times, but the breakthroughs are miracles. I am lucky enough to have witnessed such miracles continuously since this child came into my life and you will, too. The next breakthroughs came with time, but they were amazing as well.

The obsessions of our children can be interesting. You can never tell when all of the sudden the Elmo obsession will become the little rubber yellow duck or ballet shoes. It was always something with Bri, and it stayed until it had played itself out. All the interventions in the world that I tried were nothing but temporarily helpful bandages. The ballet shoes didn't come off without tears. She threw herself harshly on to the floor, and then ran away and hid in the tiniest secret corners she could find to escape. I played the game. I coaxed her out of small corners. I demanded. I reinforced approximations of behavior, which meant if she touched her ballet shoe, I would praise her!

Then, the unthinkable happened. A new occupational therapist came into the room and promptly took her shoes off and handed them to me. Then she said to Brianna, "Shoes later, time for work!" It took some restraint on my part, maybe, but also it was a lesson learned. The hardest of these lessons is the release of your power and position as the parent. I can guarantee that nobody knows your child better than you. Definitely, no person loves your child more, but that is not the issue. When it's time to push boundaries, sometimes we are not the best people to do that. The power is in your team, and your team will change throughout your journey with your child. I was blessed with amazing people throughout who taught me as a parent and as a professional. Every person on the team can have a different approach, but that's what makes the therapy work. It has different vantage points, skill sets, and styles. Your child benefits from being exposed to the full array of personalities and expectations. Don't be afraid to ask for help. Don't be afraid to listen to your heart, and follow with your instincts when it comes to your child. They belong to us, and we know every finger and every tear. We understand and see the behavior sometimes before our child does. It doesn't mean we have to do this alone.

There are some important things to remember when considering your therapy schedules. At the time when

I was taking Bri to all of her therapies, I found myself overwhelmed. She was participating in speech, occupational therapy, hippotherapy, aquatic therapy, and play therapy. I soon learned that sometimes less is more. Sometimes the intensity of therapy is needed, in certain cases. You need to evaluate your own situation with your schedule, making considerations for your child, as well as other family members, and your own personal stress level. There were times that I pulled back with the therapies. I would see Bri as a very exhausted three- or four-year-old. It all became too much for all of us, so we streamlined our sessions. I found that if I looked at her overall growth, especially with communication, that a scattered therapy schedule throughout the year was more effective for her. Take caution to understand that with children with more medical involvement or physical disabilities, the consistency of the therapy may outweigh the fatigue to some degree. It is a delicate balance that you as the parent will have to decide for your family. There are no rules. However, it is essential to listen to your child and monitor their stress levels and progress.

Therapists will progress with your child at different rates. All factors should be considered, including your own mental health. The running around the place to place is necessary, just not at the expense of living life with balance and room to enjoy your child just as they are. With that said, take note during therapies. Don't just watch and let someone else do the work, especially if this is new to you. Therapy is play at this stage. Play with the demand for language and sensory regulation. It's not anything that you can't learn and practice at home. It is essential for you and other family members to participate in home therapy. Day to day details matter, and you need to stretch the lessons to all environments.

If Bri liked a dollhouse at therapy, I used a different dollhouse at home. The big superstores had great little mommy and daddy figurines. The following week I would purchase sisters and brother figurines, pet figures, furniture, cars, and even swimming pools to add to the play. Every toy or interest is an opportunity to get the language, both receptive and expressive. The play is the work, and the work is the play, and that makes it fun. Bri used to line up everything in the dollhouse. My job was to switch it up. The highchair upstairs, the bedroom furniture in the kitchen, and it would infuriate her little self. The secret was in the fury. She wanted to put things back, and that was my opportunity to label the furniture. "Oh, you want the bed?" I would ask, and then I would request her to say "bed", then touch bed, the same old routine for getting those first words. Then I used more language as a model, "The bed goes upstairs, or the baby wants to sleep." I scripted for her, "The highchair goes in the kitchen" and whatever other verbal prompts that I could think of I said to my very eager child. The natural learning environment enables them to listen to the label and the tone of your voice. They remember, even if it is not expressed right away. Be patient. The same applied for other play. There is a type of therapy referred to as Floor time. During Floor time Therapy, the parent meets the child at the interest level of their choosing. With Bri, I did that, but I took it one step further by interrupting her obsessive play. Certainly, I started playing with what she wanted and how she wanted to build the trust. She wanted the toys or placed counting bears in a circle, and I joined her. Once it was established that we were having a great time, I made tiny redirections in our play. In general, every opportunity you have to interfere in their obsessive play, do. Now, there will be times when you should let them explore the toys, even if they are not using them functionally. The interest is the key. The more they play or explore, the more opportunities we have to use that play to incite language.

When Bri would line up her ABC Sesame Street train of four cars, it showed her cause and effect with whistling sounds. (It would make a train sound when all the pieces were together.) That was great functional play. It was educational and calming for her at the same time. Sometimes, I interfered and put the train in C-A-B order just to push the limits. I created an opportunity to develop new phrases like "my turn" and allowed her to put things back in order. I could mess it up, so to speak, to help her tolerate the unforeseen. It helped her to develop flexibility and social interaction.

"You don't always need a plan. Sometimes you just need to breathe, trust, let go and see what happens." Mandy Hale

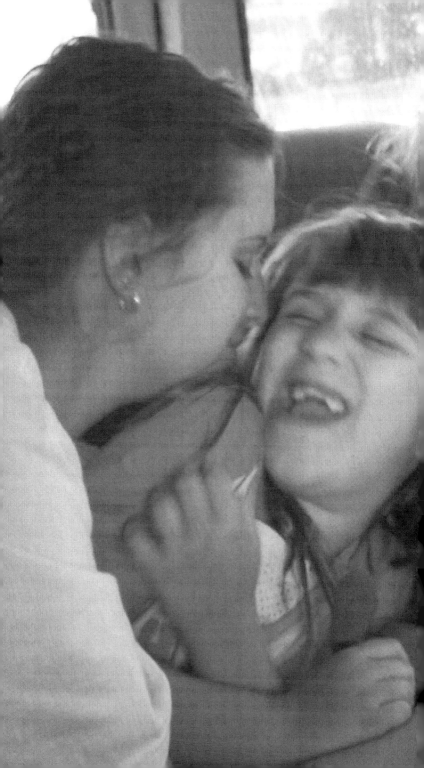

7

Do Everything

It can be frustrating to hear that every behavior must be taught. It may seem that learning behaviors should happen naturally. Well, I have been raising three girls with such different personalities that with or without special needs, the pace is unique. The catalyst for our special kids is the constant introduction to the world around them. Colors, sounds, and the tolerance of sounds and color can be so overwhelming.

To our children, the world presents all of its glory in one loud moment. All the stimulation at once, without the ability to filter between the sounds and colors. Behaviors are simply a way of protesting this bombardment of a very loud and colorful world.   To tell a child to sit quietly while they have a fabric touching them that feels like a knife for them is torture. To pay attention when the humming of the fluorescent bulbs sounds like army helicopters around them is nothing short of cruel. We couldn't do it without the typical filters we possess to discriminate between background noise and other sounds. If a child with a high sensitivity to sound demonstrates pain or fear with sound, then by all means protect them with child-sensitive headphones or even noise-canceling headphones, especially for older children. Some of our kiddos are just more sensitive, although my usual rule in my classroom is that we live in a loud world, yet there are many exceptions. Some of our children can be taught   to tune some of the extra stimuli out. There are, however, always special considerations for each child.

This world is not made up of set questions and answers, but instead try to watch, practice the difficult, and reinforce the appropriate behaviors. In other words, we have to really try to get into the heads of our kids on the spectrum and reach them where they are. Try everything, see what works, and expand on that. One example I have is going to the movies. When Bri was around three-years-old, Elana was five, and

Amanda was fourteen, it was a task to entertain all three of my girls simultaneously. The movie theatre seemed like a possibility. Bri could get through the movie, enjoy the popcorn, and almost like clockwork would begin screaming at either the best part or 10 minutes before the ending. I missed the ending of quite a few movies. I didn't want to give up this favorite pastime with my other children, so I began to practice with summer movies for children. I only took Bri if possible at times. I timed it just right so that when she was getting agitated, we would leave before the tantrum. We were done and could walk out of the theatre with some dignity. At times, I only took her to the last 15 minutes of the movie to acclimate her to staying until the end. Then, we would walk out with everybody. Of course, we went to a lot of dollar movies to be able to use the theatre for behavioral practice. We went daily in the summer. Fast forward many years, to where Bri was about 10-years-old. She actually sat through a three-hour Harry Potter movie with both of her sisters. The early work paid off. Now, Bri and I go to all kinds of events, whether a movie or a concert, and we both enjoy it.

Our children on the spectrum are like sponges. Early intervention is best, however, anytime is a time to learn new things and to scientifically light up those neurons in the brain. Neuroplasticity is a term used to describe the ability of the brain to change during a person's life. All of us, including our children, have the ability to alter our brain through new experiences and new knowledge. It's easier with most of our kids if we teach things correctly the first time and not have to retrain the brain, as in the case of behavior. Old habits can be changed, but often they are already habits and therefore must be modified. When we teach our kids the right way to behave, sit, or stay quiet in certain environments, we are giving them an advantage in the future. We start where we need to start.

One of my main regrets is that I know so much more now about raising children on the spectrum, about children in general, and about behavior. I have learned through raising my daughter, plus through tons of field experience with my career. Looking back won't change the things I wish could be changed, but I can share with you what I have learned. I refer to the home therapy, or the work, or the play. It means the same for you and your child. With every opportunity, learning takes places and patterns are made. Our children thrive on structure and patterns. Doing the same gives them the stability they need to take in the information, process it, and generalize it for their benefit. With Bri, I don't know if I said the same words, but from the crib I would go into her room and say, "Good morning, sunshine", or something to that effect with a good morning. I didn't realize it at the time, but I do now, that would be an introduction to greetings for her.

All language can be broken down into smaller steps for our kids.   It starts with receptive language, and then follows with expressive language. The target is to expose our kids to language consistently. This is true with all languages, and including those used by multilingual families.

The use of visuals or pictures is also important with single or multiple languages. The trick is using the visual supports to help the kids process the understanding of the word you are saying. Even during therapy, I had Bri working on receptively touching the requested item, ball, or Elmo, and then followed up with saying the word. I mention this quite often because it must become the way you speak to your child. Checking for understanding of the receptive language by having the child discriminate between two choices initially is preferred. If you need to take a step back and just introduce the object and label, that's fine. Hold the ball, say "touch ball". If you get no response, physically help your child touch the ball. This may seem tedious at first, but it will develop a pattern of focusing on the object and the expectation of a verbal response.

Exposure to everything is important, although there may be experiences that seem overwhelming for your child. Some events may introduce meltdowns or anxiety. During these times, take a mental note and break down the event into smaller increments. For example, if you are to attending an event with a young child with autism and you see their stress is rising, your first instinct may be to leave. That is an option. You can do that, but pay attention to where you saw the behavior change initiate. Try it again, maybe just 10 minutes later, and see if they can tolerate longer amounts of time.

I have three beautiful children. I celebrated two first birthday parties before Bri's. With her birthday, I had visions of her eating the cake face first or touching the cake, some beautiful moment that I could surely document. With Bri, an Elmo candle, and cake in my hands, I brought her to her highchair. She completely freaked out. I scrambled trying to translate her frenzy. Was it the singing? Was it the candles? Could it have been that she felt the energy and excitement in the air with the family? I couldn't discern which of these variables was ruining my fantasy of this perfect day. I couldn't be sure, but it was not as I expected.

I took away the cake and gave Bri a little taste of frosting from my finger, and let her mouth surround the sugary pleasure. I proceeded to take the Elmo and ball toppers off the cake and hand them to my screaming baby to calm her down. My theory of that event was that it was all too much for this sensory-sensitive baby. She had no previous history or experience with the whole birthday procession. All of the sudden, she had extra noise, family, and lights all around her. I had to think quickly and break down the festivities into manageable steps for her to process. The frosting was nice. Elmo was nice. Everything at the same time while strapped in a highchair may have just been too much. Tragedy was diverted temporarily, but this was before her diagnosis so interpretation of that day was a stretch for me.

Today, research shows that the implications of autism can be seen before the first birthday. Now, I see it as clear as glass. There are also theories that the baby who behaves too well, or who is calmed instantly, might be showing signs of autism. I would have thought at that time it was due to my experience as a third-time mommy. She was so readily calmed. She slept well, nursed well, and was generally just a good baby.

Unfortunately, it's easy to see things after the facts. After her diagnosis, I began to try to show her the world. The first time I took her to a puppet show at a children's theatre, she was a nervous and noisy three-year-old with tons of energy. I thought she would be entertained by Pinocchio as her sisters had been.

The first attempt, however, was a clear disaster. I don't know if it was the dark theatre or the lack of snacks allowed in the theatre, but it was not well received by my child. She wanted nothing to do with the puppet show arena. It was sad for me because it was like giving up on a family tradition that my other girls enjoyed. Determined to try it again, I hoped for a better outcome. I bought the summer membership and went often to see if it was better tolerated the next time. On one visit, I found on that Bri loved the gift shop. So, on next visit, we went only to the gift shop, and of course, purchased an item of her choosing. The visit following that, I had her participate in a walk through the puppet showroom, and then visited the gift shop.

I'm sure you get the picture. She was much younger than she is now, but all of those visits offered an opportunity to teach her about puppet shows. The same was practiced for concerts, movies, and restaurants. It took years of practice. We shared plenty of opportunities, some successful and some disasters, but all were teachable moments for both Bri and myself. I also took pictures of all of these events. It wasn't as practical as it is now with our cellphones, but I kept a camera with me at all times. The camera helped preserve our memories, as well as providing valuable visual prompts to tell her about the next event we would be going to. I also took pictures of her emotions at these events, which allowed me to talk to her about how she felt at that puppet show or wherever we were.

Don't paint the picture too perfect. It is good and helpful to show our children all of their emotions, including the negative. It's how they can communicate to us how they are feeling. It also provides an opportunity for them to predict how they might feel the next time they are at an outing. Best practice and

18 years of raising a child on the spectrum has taught me to try everything at least five times. While that statement may make you cringe as you think of an experience you had with your child that you don't care to repeat, trust me, it's worth the anguish. With my daughter, I tried everything. Some things were therapeutic and fun, and some attempts at participation in life were just humbling. I had to deal with the awkward looks at my child behaving years younger than she was in the quietest of spaces, but I dealt with it. Sometimes, I took those opportunities to provide awareness of autism to strangers. Other times, I would just leave and try to catch my breath before the next excursion. I took Bri to the movies, to the grocery store, and to church. I signed her up for gymnastics with typical peers. I registered her with her sisters to participate with the community swim team. I took her on family vacations. I lived my life with a beautiful child with autism and her sisters. It wasn't always easy. It was always a learning opportunity. Try everything. Live your life!

"We shall not cease from exploration

And the end of all our exploring

Will be to arrive where we started

And know the place for the first time."

T.S. Eliot Four Quartets

8

The Fight

At some point, the energy of fear has to be transformed into a progressive step forward for both you and your child. You can stay angry and afraid. You can blame everyone, including God. You can remain paralyzed within your limitations, or you can fight. I fought. I still fight.

I fight every day for her. I fight for autism awareness. I fight for better resources. I fight for medical research and fluid therapies. I fight for my sanity. I fight for my family. I fight for a balanced life. All of that being said, it is not an easy task.

This is how I feel as a parent. As a teacher, my fierceness was no less, but I was not as vulnerable as with my own child until I shared both positions. Then I understood the urgency to fight for all of our kids, at all times.

I remember an incident on a field trip, or technically a community- based instructional trip, with my class of middle-schoolers. Circumstances arose where I ended up restraining a bigger kid during a mall trip. Public onlookers watched me interact with this student, having no idea what I was doing. I wondered in hindsight if I had my identification badge on to document my profession. I wondered if the police would be called soon by some concerned citizen.

I felt such mortification for the student and not for myself. I knew what I was doing. I understood that it was a meltdown most likely over not being able to buy something from his favorite music store. He worked through it with my prompts and recovered nicely, enabling us to move on. The looks on the strangers' faces were unnerving, even though my actions were part my profession and the child was my student. I began to explain autism to anyone within earshot. I calmly stated that this was not a behavior, but a sensory meltdown. I said this child was a good boy, and although much taller than me, he would not intentionally hurt me and would calm down shortly. He may have looked aggressive at that moment, but I knew he was scared, overcome with frustration and other emotions, and completely unable to express it. My explanation was maybe helpful, but it was also irritating that more of the public don't understand our kids. We've come a long way with awareness due to organizations like Autism Speaks and the Autism Society, and other amazing foundations. Yet, there is more work to be done.

At times, I carried small business cards that listing an explanation of behaviors that might be exhibited by our students on the spectrum. I randomly passed them out if the occasion merited it. In all of these professional experiences, I came to realize very strongly that our kids don't like these meltdowns any more than we do. It's a frightening and out-of-control experience for them.

So many of the children with autism who have crossed my path in my classroom have shown aggression. They bit, kicked, screamed, spit, and pinched us for hours if they were allowed. Then, slow silent tears fell, and even one particular student saying, "Sorry, Ms. Lynn, no bite", so apologetically. It is heartbreaking to think of a child so out of control with their neurological systems that they aren't able to voice their frustration in any other way but to use their bodies. They don't want to. They hate it. They even know it isn't the right way, but they can't help it. It can be a spiral of communication deficits versus physical and mental confusion. This combination creates the perfect storm for our kids. A meltdown can be very intimidating for both a student and teacher, and heartbreaking for parent and child, and even for the general public who are exposed to it. However, we can try to educate the population one step at a time through various venues. The main point is that a meltdown, or any display of behavior that is concerning to you or the child, should be respected. It can be analyzed and made to be as comfortable as possible through the process. For example, allow the child to have some space if needed and if elopement is not a concern. Do not try to talk a child through a meltdown unless they are physically calm and ready.

They will not hear your words.

Think of it like this, for any person who may be tired or frustrated, or not tolerant of loud noises or allergens, or just in a generally bad mood, when asked to perform at their best will fall short. We all have these weaknesses from time to time, but our children on the spectrum face this every day. Every moment without the ability to filter out the extrasensory bombardment of visual, auditory, or tactile invasions is beyond difficult.

I remember listening to Temple Grandin at a conference. She is a professor of animal science at Colorado State University. She is also on the spectrum. She mentioned that to ask a child with autism to give their name on request is the equivalent of a neurotypical person being asked the same, but first having to complete a calculus equation and then to retrieve their name.

The work in retrieving language as simple as a request to say their names can be excruciating at times. Sometimes, it can be rote and ready. On-demand retrieval of basic information can seem so easy, but it is not. Consider the amount of filtering our kids have to go through when ruling out the extra sounds, the touch, and the visual stimuli, and then produce language. It's exhausting work that they must go through daily.

It's not surprising that at times they present the need to shut down on intervals just to gather their strength. In homes and classrooms, there should be space, or several spaces, to enable your child to seek out shelter from sensory overload. As you learn about your child's sensory needs, you will see where they seek refuge out the most. It could be a place to calm down and stay in a quiet covered area just to recover. It could be a crash pad or a bed. It could be a chair that they plunge their bodies into with full force. The reason for this is that they need to feel their own under- stimulated bodies in space and motion.

We went through several expensive all-wood bedframes with Bri. Beds that had survived the two other children just fine. Then along comes this little energizer bunny who crashes, jumps, and breaks two-inch wooden slats in the bed until it's no longer functional. The same could be said for various pieces of furniture throughout her young years.

I spent hours upon hours with three kids at the park. In between the swings and the climbing equipment, I tried to get her energy focused. At the time, I didn't realize the full impact of her sensory needs. The swing offered proprioceptive input that her body demanded. In the natural environment, the park can be a great place to help your child regulate their sensory needs in between therapy sessions. Depending on the nature of the child's needs, it can be helpful to organize their play. For example, try the slide then a climb, and then swing, and then repeat to systematically organize their bodies. All of this can be determined in a more specific sensory diet plan from your occupational therapist.

For home therapy assistance, there are many resources for sensory equipment that can be used in the home especially at the younger stage. I always kept a miniature trampoline in the living room along with a large yoga ball. I tried to mimic the therapy sessions we had with our occupational therapist. You can get creative with your traditional swing set by ordering different sensory-based styles of swings. I used a flat swing called a platform swing with Bri when she was younger. She would switch off with pure joy from a typical swing or a bucket swing, and then the platform swing. It would help her organize her body and make her spirit happy.

There are tire swings, standing swings, and many other accessories that will help you build your own therapeutic backyard. As she grew older, I purchased a full-sized trampoline for outside. I wish now that I had bought that for her whole childhood. It has provided hours of sensory fun and regulation for her.

The occupational therapist turned out to be a shift changer for Bri. In that world, I was educated on all of the functions of their bodies and how such equipment can assist them. I thought, although that the speech therapist would have played a bigger role with a communication disorder. They were both, however, immeasurably essential to our team.

The occupational therapist for Bri was able to show me her issues with gravitational fear. I could never change her diapers on a traditional changing table. She would shriek as if in sheer panic even as in infant. Obviously, I had no idea why in those days, but as her mother I knew she hated it. I therefore changed her on the floor or on the bed where I sat next to her. This was pure instinct as a mother because I surely hadn't been expecting autism in my young daughter.

Initially on the platform swing with the occupational therapist, Bri demonstrated tremendous fear, which surprised me because she loved swings. In all the way their bodies betray them with balance, anxiety, control, it still can be surprising to them and to us as caretakers. Each of these sensory deficits can be aided with the help of a good occupational therapist with the side benefit being language. As Bri's body became more regulated with her sensory needs, language came more readily. It all works together, and is another reason it's so important to have communication between your team members. You need the entire team to see your child, as each will see a different area of need.

It is much more cohesive to have a team in place. You waste less time, and everyone benefits from the input from all areas of expertise.   I am still surprised when I'm in my classroom and working on a difficult task for a child, and one of my therapists enters with a different technique and the child masters it. Everyone brings their personality and skills to the table, but it's all different, and the child benefits. not be a cookie-cutter formula for any child. You must advocate for your child. Don't choose a battle for the sake of something that won't really affect your child's educational performance. Know your child, and have your facts ready to present to the team that best represents your child's strengths and weaknesses. Try to be a team player, and hopefully, you'll have a team that wants to do the same. You are your child's first teacher and therapist, and you know best what they can and cannot do. Bring to your meetings notes from private evaluations or their therapists and documentation in the form of videos that represent your child's usual behavior and skill sets.

A bridge between home and school is essential to provide the best outcome for everyone involved. Often during early intervention evaluations, it is not always the true assessment of a child's abilities. These evaluations can provide a good baseline of presenting behaviors. In other words, a therapist coming in to work with a child for a few hours or less is obviously not going to see everything your child can do. Babies or young children by nature do not perform for strangers.

Children usually don't perform all of their tricks in this restrictive environment. Such evaluations can provide a start to see any red flags in their development. They're an opportunity to measure basic developmental milestones and get a good family history.

"Love recognizes no barriers. It jumps hurdles, leaps fences, penetrates walls to arrive at its' destination full of hope." Maya Angelou

9

The Sensory Signs

The autism world is getting bigger daily. For some reasons, it can be a good thing. Awareness, research, and resources are expanding. Opportunities for our kids to fit into the world are growing. I remember sitting in one of Brianna's first Individual Education Plan meetings feeling very apprehensive but confident at the same time because I had run hundreds of these meetings myself as a teacher. I had asked for opportunities with the public school. Now, I am a public-school teacher. I believe in public schools with all my heart. My children attend public school.

Unfortunately, the Individual Education Plan table can be a place of contradictions. Decisions are made on a relevant school model, not a medical or therapeutic model. Limitations will be placed on families. If there are burning issues for your child, you must advocate for them. Decisions that are made due to budget concerns, staff reductions, or classroom space are not acceptable and should not be tolerated. Push back will often be necessary in those cases.

Having a true assessment of your child is vital to know what services your child will need. It's called an Individual Education Plan for a reason. It should As the parent, you are the voice for your child, especially during   an assessment. While it may be tempting in these situations to overinflate or underinflate your child's abilities, it isn't necessary. Where your child is developmentally will present for the most part.

A trained evaluator will recognize the signs for focus, tolerance, and interest that the child is exhibiting with the testing materials. In addition, your input as a parent is invaluable. Do not be shy or worried about speaking up. If the evaluator does not see a performance, but you know your child can do it, for example with a puzzle or stacking blocks, then by all means provide the information.

You and your evaluator are trying to create a picture

together to see where your child would benefit from support. If you've had other children like I have before your child with special needs, then the differences may stand out for you. Sometimes if your first or only child has developmental delays, you may not recognize them right away when you don't have another child to compare to. In my case, when Bri was so behind in language, after all of my excuses I realized there was a delay. It didn't stand out like a beacon; it was subtle. She was a picky eater. She had a startle reflex for a very long time. She had sensory regulation deficits.

When Bri was two-years-old, we went to the beach for a family vacation. Her delight at seeing the water and the crashing waves at her baby feet was a sight to see. Giggles and chasing waves were a very typical and sweet behavior for a baby seeing the ocean for the first time. She looked just like my other two children during their first visits to the beach. The difference came when she would run up and down the beach without abandon. Running and laughing, then running and laughing more until she was crying and I caught up with her. I was so concerned about the tears. I picked up my toddler, only to have her fall asleep immediately in my arms. I was a bit confused and concerned due to the fact that she never napped. She didn't fall asleep immediately like that under usual circumstances. Not knowing what had happened, I let her sleep. I put her into the baby carrier, on a blanket, and covered it with the rainbow umbrella. I thought the whole behavior was strange. Later, I would understand that she had sensory regulation deficits. Her body had been out of control while running, and she was unable to stop on her own. It was as if her body was on a scale of zero to ten with no fives in the middle. She simply couldn't slow down or stop. Not until the tears came to let me as her parent know that something was wrong. The immediate shutting down through sleep was her body's way of saying that is enough!

I came to understand through this event that I would need to intervene in helping her regulate her little body because she was not capable of doing so on her own. Her system was off. The balance in fast and slow, calming, exciting, all-around regulating was not under control, so it had to be undermined. It meant the locating of little tents, tunnels, cozy chairs, bean bag chairs, little trampolines, swings, weighted blankets, and vests—all sensory equipment that could help her regulate. It meant an endless search for better parks for her to play at. By better, I mean fenced in, so I could keep her safe and contained when she wanted to run away.

Sometimes, I would take her to an open soccer field and just let her run like the wind. She was little, but she was fierce at that age. Her need to run freely without limitations was so necessary for her but exhausting for me. I would ask her sisters to run with her. They would tire out before the "baby." At that time, I felt that she would grow up to be an amazing athlete.

My father was a track and field star at the University of Miami. At his passing, he was still in the University of Miami's Hall of Fame. I humored myself that she had inherited his athletic prowess.

The serious side of sensory regulation for our kids is that their bodies are foreign to them while in that state. It's not comfortable to want to run without stopping. Neither is not having the energy to get out of the bed. I imagine it's how I feel when I overdo the expresso! I worked hard to read her body.   I methodically structured her bedtime to ensure she was sleeping well, exercising in balance, and calm in her general mood.

Each child is different. Sensory regulation changes as they grow. Music can be very helpful in regulating, as it can be controlled. In my classroom and with my own child, I implement music into our day. I play fun, loud, and fast music for about two songs, and then shift to a slower song. I model slower hand movements to calm down their bodies. There is even some wonderful sensory-based music that caters to just this kind of therapeutic approach. It has words to help the child understand to speed up or slow down to the song. There are also songs that are specific to teaching necessary skills such as following directions or waiting in line.

Children remember best to music as well as understand the concept when presented musically. When combined with visual prompts—pictures to represent the vocabulary of the song—children are able to learn at a faster pace. In my day-to-day teaching, if there is a task, there's a song to go with it. This was, and still is, definitely true for my own daughter as well. Music is magic for all of our kids. Its therapeutic power is immeasurable. All of the tools and strategies that we learn from occupational therapy, speech therapy, music, and art are to be our tools to use as well. You will develop a personal program for your child that will help in numerous ways and will help your child feel more balanced and in control. You should always be looking out for signs of agitation before it begins. When you start to see their anxiety rising or find them just generally not at ease, you may want to try some of your strategies. Best practices for a sensory diet are to use it proactively like an antibiotic on a scheduled regimen. Have a plan for high- and low-energy activities throughout the day. It's what I try to put into place in my classroom—a plan. Life sometimes doesn't allow a plan. When reality hits, like it did with my own child when I was in the middle of some errand and I saw her anxiety rise, I tried one of the strategies. You have two ways to make this happen. Try and plan for a consistent way to include an interval of high and low activities when you can. For the other times, knowing a few targeted calming activities that work almost every time for your child can be utilized.

I could sing to Bri a favorite song, and she usually redirected her energy. I could go faster with the stroller or shopping cart if I were in the store. I could pick her up and sway with her or rock her a little to calm. As she grew, I always tried to have sugarless gum in my purse for her to chew as it can calm and distract. Of course, I had to have a whole pack of gum for that, because she would swallow the gum quite rapidly.

I chose my battles because I needed to finish the shopping or whatever my task was, and I just wanted to steal a few more minutes of sanity. At these times, an introduction of a new strategy like swinging, spinning, or jumping can change the mood and the physical uneasiness the child may be experiencing. If they're active or overly active, it's time to switch to a calming activity. Take a nice walk or practice walking on a sidewalk curb or a beam to help work on their balance and focus. It's also a great distractor to give them a new physical challenge like walking on uneven surfaces or on the curb.

It's a constant puzzle for sure, but you can become a master at interpreting your child's sensory needs in a very short time. Just be a good observer of their body language, verbal output, and energy. They communicate to us using this information, and we must be diligent to pay attention to the smallest of details. What does sensory look like in a young child, especially a baby? In my personal experience with Brianna, it looked like anything and everything   in her little pudgy hands went into her hair. To this day, Bri has the thickest hair, enough for several little girls.

I attribute it to the chocolate pudding, baby food, and anything else she had that went directly to the top of her little brunette head. I think once, something soft, squishy, and somewhat foreign was in her hands and it had to go straight to her hair, as if in some mad attempt to get it off of her hands.

Now on some less pleasant moments—little bitty diapers. While I was still well into denial about anything being different with her, there were a couple of occasions that shocked me as I came into quite a mess in the crib! Upon having a messy diaper, she must have tried to get at the culprit of her discomfort and spread the contents all over the walls, crib railings, bedding, everywhere. Panicking and cleaning everything up with bleach as fast as I could, I tried to make sense of this behavior that with child number three was completely new to me. This was in addition to the accompaniment of two other children shouting how gross everything was! Luckily, as a mother faced with a crisis, we go right into multi-tasking and clean up the mess, clean up the baby, and calm the other children. I can assure you that I knew nothing of how to translate any of these behaviors in my little devilish imp.

She was precious in every way, and occasionally she would throw me something crazy to handle. I had no way of interpreting it because I did not want to at that time. It took me many years,   with the knowledge of hindsight and the complete education from occupational therapist colleagues, to understand the significance of the sensory needs being demonstrated through all of these acts.

As a side note, when diapers were dumped and spread throughout the bedding and crib, I did, as a typical parent, use this opportunity to teach her, "No!" She was a baby. I didn't blame her, but I didn't want a recurrence of said behavior. I just said, "No touch, diapers on."   It was silly because she was so very little, but I needed to tell her. I think she was listening, because it didn't happen again. Either she was listening or I was much faster and more observant. Either way, it needed to be a one-time event.

Sensory interest or defensiveness can present in many different ways. In my preschool teaching experiences, there have been a lot of little babies that don't want anything to do with art materials. Where most kids delight in shaving cream, finger paint, or even modeling clay, there are some that want nothing to do with it. Before the initial attempt at even touching it, they will refuse to participate even a little.

As a teacher of the little ones, I know how important it is for them to touch it. It is essential to give that first feel, smell, and even taste. To get them to become familiar with these school activities, there has to be contacted. Where does the resistance come from? Sometimes, it's about lack of experience or exposure. It can be that they've never seen it before. It could be that the smell is too strong for them. It's often about the texture. In these cases, it is best to let the child approach the materials on their own.

First, I stage the table and the materials, making it highly attractive with colors, toys, modeling clay, and cutouts for them to explore. Next, I put on some nice calming music and just let nature take its course. If a child went near the table and touched the materials, I quietly sat next to them without any prompting and just played next to them, which usually gave them an opportunity to explore at their own pace. I only intervened to prevent the eating of nonedible materials.

Strategies exist for those darlings that put everything in their mouths. With these particular kids, I used many substitutes, such as whip cream instead of shaving cream or paint made with gelatin and whipped cream. In addition, there are also many fantastic modeling clay or dough recipes that are deliciously edible.

The problem with our children on the spectrum is the generalization of concepts. If you start out with edible products then introduce the traditional concepts, it's hard for them to discriminate the difference. The reverse is even true. Our children tend to learn things one way, and altering it can make it confusing. That's not to say that it can't be done—it must be done.

Generalization in all areas is essential to expanding their understanding of the world around them. It simply must be taught with careful thought of where you are and what your next step is.

One of the more popular therapies is within the realm of Applied Behavior Analysis or ABA. A part of this therapy is discrete trial therapy, or in other words, activities that are taught in small increments. For example, if you want a child to put a puzzle piece into a puzzle, you can give them a three-piece puzzle and a pegged chunky puzzle piece, and see what they do with it. Maybe they will complete it all on their own, without any instruction, which happens quite often as our children are so visual. They have an uncanny ability to see and complete it without the typical trial and error that most toddlers will attempt. With the discrete trial, you hand the child one puzzle piece at a time, and depending on their action, put them through a series of least restrictive prompts to encourage them to complete the puzzle or start by placing one piece in the puzzle. If an effort is not made initially, the therapist or trained parent will verbally direct, gesture in the right direction, touch their hand, physically move their hand, or completely help the child hand over hand to ensure success. The prompting hierarchy ranges from least to most, as needed. It's a very effective therapy process with the generalization of skills, and then the maintenance of those learned skills. It's a process that cycles from beginning to end, then continues again in fewer details but keeps the same framework.

Generalization is key, and it also works in reverse. It involves us spending the time to teach language concepts, such as the vocabulary of a ball. A ball can be big, small, red, or blue, and for some of our kids this can be very confusing. They may only learn that the ball in their hand, which happens to be small and red, is the only definition of a ball for them. We then must stretch that interpretation. During the beginning of discrete trial therapy, the format may need to be taught like that. First, we start with labeling the ball for the child. Then, we have the child touch the ball to show receptive understanding. Next, we encourage the child to repeat the label and verbalize on his own by saying, "Say ball." We then repeat the process. Once understood, or if conceptualized immediately, the introduction of other balls then takes place with the same labeling.

As far as language, steps can be taken to enhance the sentence length by adding adjectives to the concept. For example, the ball is described as a blue ball or big ball. The ball's description expands when the child is ready. Working with a good speech therapist to enhance language development and continuous practice at home will help build the basic vocabulary. Language development must be practiced around the clock to have the child hear the language, practice the language, and use it.

Generalization can also happen in reverse when the child translates information to overgeneralize. An example of this may be that once a child is taught how to eat something, then everything goes into their mouth. Another example would be a child learns to draw or paint on paper, then he overgeneralizes and draws or paints on walls, furniture, and other places.

When Bri was about four-years- old, she showed no sign of understanding letters except to sing her alphabet song. She wasn't even pointing to letters or labeling letters, or demonstrating a receptive understanding of letters. She'd put a letter puzzle together rather quickly, and again I took it to be sign of visual strength and not actual letter recognition.

We had been living in our house for about 15 years, and as home projects go, my bedroom was the last on the priority list with three little girls to raise. One summer, my husband hired a painter, and I very carefully chose a beautiful blue-grey color to paint my master bedroom. It was a lovely, calming color like the night sky at dusk.

It looked so nice for about two weeks. Then one day I walked in after shopping at the grocery store and having left Bri at home with her sisters. I discovered that my newly painted walls were graffitied with two-foot letters in red sharpie, spelling out "Elmo's World" with the apostrophe included! Remember what I said about seeing miracles every day? Who taught her how to write or read? I couldn't believe what I was seeing. It took me quite a while to realize that my beautiful wall had a new décor, but it was okay.

Believe it or not, the discovery of new skills that I had no idea that she possessed was worth losing the vanity of my freshly painted walls. Yes, I grabbed the camera and took a picture. I called her grandmother, and I cried. No tears for my room, but for my beautiful little self-taught genius.

A new therapy meant more work to be done, concentrating on the alphabet, reading, and writing. Always asking the question "What do I do next?" with her understanding new concepts. Truthfully, I will always be asking that question, and you should be, too. There are no limitations to what they can learn. There are only new horizons to uncover how to teach them.

"Once we accept our limits, we go beyond them."

Albert Einstein

10

Real Life

Now, don't let me lead you on that I handled every adventure with grace and humor.

I had my real-life moments on more occasions than I would have preferred. I am still learning how to accept the crazy days and all the extra work that comes with those as well, usually at the most inopportune moment. I am constantly working on the elusive balance of life that we all struggle to find even for a short time. That being said, there was one time in particular that I will tell you about.

The Story of the Blue Dog

When Bri was about five-years-old, I decided that we need a puppy. I was working in a school where one of our monthly visitors was from Canine Assistants. They would come in with a cartload of puppies that were the cutest, well-trained, little bundles of joy. Mostly they were Golden Retriever puppies, with some Labradors in the mix. My elementary school–aged students were allowed to touch them, which brought them immeasurable delight. I began a six- month search into professionally trained dogs, especially those for children with disabilities, to work as a service dog. The expense for this kind of dog was way over our budget, and the wait list was years long. However, I did some research on my own and started to look for a breeder. After all, I thought, if I had a degree or two specializing in behavior management, couldn't I train a puppy?

We found the perfect family and went to the house when the puppies were eight-weeks-old. Our little Josie chose our family. She went straight to my middle daughter, much to her pleasure. A deal was made, and we went home with the sweetest pup. She was an amazing puppy with blonde fur and big round tummy, and we all quickly fell in love. She'd been in our home a mere couple of months when Bri went out the front door on her own. It was unusual behavior for her, but behaviors change quickly with our kids on the spectrum. So out toddles this little girl with autism and following right behind her without a leash is our Josie! Of course, I was right behind both of them, but that's not to say that I wasn't amazed at the discipline and instinct of this new puppy. It had been a love affair ever since for our entire family and anyone who met this new family member. A companion dog is a good therapy option, but consider it carefully for your family. Like any pet, it's also a lot of work.

One special night brings me to the point of my story. I had been painting with Bri over the summer. I was working on her creativity and exploring different art materials and generally just having fun with her. I had put her to bed that night and settled into what I imagined would be my adult time to relax. There's no such thing   in our world for the most part. I had just purchased a new camera, and I was trying to put batteries into it, read the directions, and just was pretty caught up in this project. Meanwhile, I hear screaming from my other daughters. I looked up to see what the commotion was all about. The dog, our Josie, at that time about 45 pounds, was completely covered in blue tempera paint! I wish I had the whereabouts to have my camera ready and take a picture of this chaos! I didn't, however, and it was before cellphones. Needless to say, panic took over. Decisions to be made were twofold. Who did I clean up first? I had a very excited puppy covered in blue, running all over my Persian carpet. I had a blue child with autism, who was laughing and also covered in paint. It was not one of my finer moments. It wasn't cute or funny. It was a disaster! Due to my disposition at the time, I chose to wash the dog first! I took Josie upstairs to my bathroom, stuck her in the bath, which wasn't to her pleasure, and got her cleaned up. Meanwhile, I order Bri's sisters to not let Bri out of the highchair until I could get to her. I ended up cleaning my house until well after midnight. I would like to believe that I remember this story fondly, but that may be a stretch. There will be moments like this with any children, but with Bri it just seemed to be so much more involved. All of these opportunities or disasters, though, can be a chance for learning. As much as I wish I had pictures of that day, it's permanently seared into my brain due to the impact it made on my living room. For months, I was finding evidence of blue in various parts of my house. The learning, or concept, that I would hope to become understood by Bri was that we love painting. Art and painting are something so fun that we can enjoy, but there is a time and a place for everything, which took the freedom out of my little artist's hands. It was necessary for the next few days following the blue storm for me to teach her the appropriate way to paint, where we keep our supplies, where we paint, and what we do not paint.

I taught her to brush the dog. I let her help me feed the dog. Our language concepts circled around puppy care and that we don't paint Josie because she doesn't like it. My advice in these situations is to try and enjoy the crazy moments. See them for what they are, but for your own sanity develop your sense of humor during those times. If you are too uptight, your stress level will soar, and so will your child's. In each teachable moment, you'll come to a new understanding of your child. Take each opportunity, good or bad, messy or near catastrophic, and view it from a distance when you can. Analyze the pre- and post-action, and see what you can do differently next time to avoid the unforeseeable. Our blue dog is a precious memory for me, one that we all survived. Carpets will clean up for the most part. My family won't forget that night. Hopefully, I was able to take a fiasco and turn it into how Bri graduated to a new level of understanding about several areas.

The generalization of concepts is never-ending. As we work with our children, we are teaching them the vocabulary of the world around them, step by step. In the beginning, we teach language to give a simple name to an object we hold. Bri learned the few words she knew and kept those words for herself forever. Although in her toddler years, her only words were Elmo, ball, no, and mommy, she used that small inventory of language to describe her world. She would walk around with one baby hand holding a small ball and the other holding Elmo. Mommy was the person who followed her around, fed her, and kept her safe. Mommy was a good word to know. She called me and showed me the two hands. She showed me the ball, repeating the word "ball" several times, then look at her other hand, and say "no, no ball". She said "Elmo" then showed me Elmo, then called my name and repeated these phrases. I redirected her away from the perseveration. These lessons were more than vocabulary. These lessons are their way to begin to navigate their surroundings. Each object that's labeled and understood in expressive and receptive language, and the ability to say it and understand it, becomes their own. Even when Bri only had possession of her favorite words, she was able to communicate the things that were most important to her.

The same is true for generalizations of activities. Language grows and develops into a working vocabulary. Activities expand into what they do and how they do it. Everything doesn't have to fit tightly into a little box, but in the mind of our kids, there needs to be a compartmentalized way of doing things.

They learn to see patterns this way.

When I taught Bri that we only use paint at the table and on paper, it was helpful to her. When she understood that we don't write on mommy's bedroom walls or any walls, she learned we would have fewer surprises. When I introduced a big butcher paper for her to reveal her innermost artist, I realized that I could have a cleaner rug. When I taught her that the dog needs grooming, feeding, and playing with, but we don't paint her, knowledge was gained for both of us.

These wonderful things I learned through very interesting experiences. As much as our children need the opportunity to generalize what they learn so they are not limited, it also serves   us well to discourage self-limiting or discrimination of what they don't want to explore. This concept pertains to everything, including food. Our children are consistently picky eaters. As a parent, you may have already witnessed the tight window our children give us as far as preferred food choices. For the sake of generalization and discrimination, it's pertinent to attempt to introduce new foods on a regular basis, especially from a young age, as you have an advantage before habits set in. Label the food and its color. Describe the flavor to enhance the eating experience whenever possible. There will be times where any new item, food or otherwise, won't be tolerated and get to within an inch of our children's faces. They know what they like and what they don't. The challenge is in expanding those horizons in every area possible.

I remember very well how Bri discriminated among all of her little Disney figurines. She decided which made the cut to stay in her play area. Sadly, there were many unloved characters, including Tigger that was flushed several times. Winnie-the-Pooh did make it to the favorite list on most occasions. There is never a shortage of teachable moments. Every morning, you and your child will begin a new day of discovering the world.

"Sometimes you will never know the value of a moment, until it becomes a memory." *Dr. Seuss*

11

Diet and Picky Eaters

The most frustrating part of self-limiting with our children is probably in the area of eating. Eating is the most basic of human pleasure and survival. Yet, eating is the most common problem with our children on the spectrum. They not only self-limit by nature of their disability, but they won't even try new things without having some very big tantrums.

I nursed Bri for as long as I could, mainly because I knew she would be my last baby to nurse, and I loved it. I fed her to bond with and nourish her for the most months possible. It was 18 months before I weaned her completely. I also fed her cereal and baby food at the appropriate developmental stages because she had a very good appetite. As far as baby food, she was a captive audience, so I didn't have much resistance at that age. In fact, she ate her pureed food quite well. She did seem to have a definite craving for ice cream and chocolate at an early age, but so did her sisters. I never paid too much attention to it, because she was growing and healthy. She seemed to be getting all the nutrition she needed, especially with breast milk.

As we started delving into our therapies more and I read more about nutrition, supplements, and special diets, I became confused about her dietary needs. So much information exists about diets for our children that it can be quite daunting. A book by Lisa Lewis titled *Special Diets for Special Kids* gives more specifics that can be very helpful to your child's individual needs. I advise starting with a developmental pediatrician or nutritionist specializing in this area to plan your own diet for your child.

Medical tests can also determine specific digestive disorders, allergies or sensitivities to certain foods specific to your case. Good information is available, but it can be extremely overwhelming. Do your own research and make your own decision with your child's team. Alternative diets are much easier these days with so many chain stores providing gluten-free options and various baking flours, but it can still be cumbersome to find the right products for your needs.

Bri wasn't showing any of the telltale signs for gluten or casein sensitivity. Still, I was a mother willing to try anything and everything, so we did. For six months, I took her off of all bread and milk when she was about three-years-old.

We had just gone on vacation, and we were in a play area at the mall. Both of my little ones became violently ill with a terrible stomach virus. While recovering at grandma's house, I kept both of my girls away from any milk products. I thought I saw something with Bri's development. I saw her toe-walking behavior stop. Her language increased. She was more animated. What had changed? I thought about all the variables that could have brought on a positive change. Then I remembered that for at least 10 days due to the stomach virus, neither of my children digested any milk products of any kind.

I questioned myself profusely. Could Bri have a casein

or lactose sensitivity? Could I have been nursing her for more than a year and a half, thinking I was helping her but actually hurting her instead? I agonized over the potentiality. Mothers tend to blame themselves first and feel the guilt even when we shouldn't. I'm that mother. I went to the pediatrician for some answers. They said there was no definitive test for her. She didn't have the signs of the leaky gut syndrome, which some kids on the spectrum do develop. She did have some constipation issues, but the suggestions were always to add more water and fruit to her diet. Hence, I took it upon myself to go full-fledged into a gluten- and casein-free lifestyle with my daughter.

I changed her bread and gave her no more ice cream, milk, yogurt, or cheese. It was difficult and expensive. I am no baker, but I attempted to become a gluten- free baker. The resistance from Bri was ridiculous as we persevered. The problem with a new diet being introduced to most children who I've encountered in my experience (and especially Bri) is that if they don't recognize or want a new food, they will hold out. By this, I mean it was all or nothing with her. I was a mom—I was not good with this holding-out behavior. I begged her to try something, to eat something, and she simply refused. Her self-limiting expanded. She'd eat tons of watermelon or grapes and drink water. Then, she would show her determination not to try anything else and refuse to eat. It was beyond torture for me, and I am sure for her as well.

Food can be such a great reinforcer for our kids when they like an item. Speech therapists and teachers often use edible treats to elicit language from our kids all of the time. When you have a child on a restricted diet, these options need to be very creative. Luckily, there are healthier choices in most stores, and you can find viable options.

The bottom line for Bri was that after six months of this diet change, there were no more significant changes. For my child during that period, the diet didn't seem to be influencing her language development or behavior anymore after those initial signs. At that juncture, I decided to slowly add some milk products back into her diet. I followed that up very carefully with wheat products, monitoring any behavioral changes closely. The general consensus is that when a child is suffering from dietary sensitivities or allergens, then the behavioral changes can be seen almost immediately over the course of a few weeks.

Providing healthy food and the best nutrition possible for all kids is always best. Everyone benefits from shopping locally and organically whenever possible. The farm-to-table concept is increasing in popularity in most places, or some of us are lucky enough to know where the actual farms are. Gathering our own food that comes from the Earth and sharing it with our friends and family is definitely something for which we should strive. With our children and their picky palates, the best way is to keep food fresh and simple. Introduce two colors at once, but maybe don't mix them. The children who love everything separated will feel more comfortable and are more likely to try the food you are offering. Remember to introduce a new fruit or bread one item a time for interest and to determine possible allergies. I encourage you to monitor any rashes, behavior, and other concerns with your pediatrician. For our family, I tried to reduce the gluten when I could and slowly introduced a more typical diet.

"Life is a succession of lessons which must be lived to be understood." Helen Keller

12

Health Concerns

As far as diet and other physical manifestations with our children with autism, it can be difficult to keep up because the issues change often and sometimes seem to show up, out of nowhere. Constipation is a pretty common ailment with our kids. I know there are various connections to stress and abdominal issues, as well as diet. Sufficient input of liquids to hydrate their bodies is vital. Some parents have suffered through so many different digestive issues with their children. All digestive issues should be shared with your pediatrician. I don't say that just as a disclaimer, but out of urgency due to the fact that our children cannot communicate their early symptoms, and we must be predictors of their bodily afflictions, if any.

Bri didn't really start to have intestinal issues until she became more selective with her diet. The problems began with all of her self- limiting and avoidance of trying new foods and even eating healthy choices. She would go a day or two and not go to the bathroom, which was a huge concern to me. I increased her water and fruit intake, and even gave her baby massages in hopes of stimulating her little system.

Around age five, she started a new behavior during one of those irregularly scheduled times of elimination. She began poking herself in the back with her little fingers. I moved her hands down and tried to get some communication from her to see what the problem was. We must be super investigators and observers of any new or strange behaviors. We must try our best to derive a little piece of information from every curious situation. I told her to stop and moved her hands down, interpreting her poking to be some random self-inflicting behavior. I truthfully had no idea why she was doing it or how to stop it.

I didn't see any insect bite or anything on her back that would cause alarm. After a few days of this new behavior, I noticed that all of this poking herself with such force caused small circular bruises all over her back from her little fingertips. It was horrifying! My little baby had poked bruises into her back until she was covered with black and blue dots.

I took her straight to the developmental pediatrician and explained to him the last few days' worth of behaviors. I looked to him for an immediate solution. I was frightened by this behavior because she had never shown any signs of aggression or self-injury behavior, but many of our children do. She was frustrated and in pain, and I was a mother with no answers to help my child.

Her doctor, Dr. Leslie Rubin, my hero, sent us straight to the hospital for a stomach X-ray. I am a behaviorist by trade and her poking looked like a behavior to me. I was not putting two and two together. The doctor requested images of her abdomen, which showed a severe blockage in her bowels. Basically, she was holding her bowel movements. She went to the bathroom just enough, yet not all the way to efficiently cleanse her intestines.

Over time, it made her sick and definitely caused her pain. Her only way of communication to me was to poke herself until bruising to show me that she was in pain. We don't even need to discuss how frustrating this is for a parent. It is obvious. Your child that cannot tell you the simplest of health issues, and especially describe their pain or even the location of it.

It's heart-wrenching, and sometimes, it just doesn't seem to end. There's always something they need to tell us and they can't. We, as parents, do our best on a constant basis to interpret their message, but often it takes time. The summary of this doctor's visit was that she needed medication to help loosen her stools and stabilize her system for a while. It helped to make her more regular with her bathroom needs, which seemed easy enough.

I have more information on potty training in upcoming chapters, but at this stage of Bri's life she was potty trained and independent with her self- care, which was very important and crucial to her moving forward in all environments. With the introduction of this medicine, a couple of new obstacles then presented. Her little tummy was out of control; the dosage was too strong for her. Although she was independent in the bathroom, under this stressful attack on her system, a problem arose.

I walked into the bathroom only to see that my precious little girl was trying so desperately to clean up after herself with all the guest towels. Truthfully, I wasn't concerned about the mess at all, but I was heartbroken for this little angel who was trying so hard to take care of herself. She had been successfully potty trained for years, yet in this situation, her body betrayed her. A quick call to the doctor remedied the issue with a change in the dosage amount and an intermittent schedule of medicine. The simple can be so complex in our world. Problems that just don't seem as big with a typical child are magnified with ours.

We are their voice. It is up to us to disseminate the layers of whatever goes wrong.

A simple tummy ache in either of my other two

children would have been resolved so quickly and differently. For my youngest, it was bruises and pain, X-rays, and a brief loss of independence. I can tell you how difficult these things can be, especially if you let them overtake you. I never really had time to think about the details. I was just a mom, a mom in action, determined to help Bri develop into a happy, healthy, little girl.

"Everybody is worth everything."

Maya Angelou

13

Potty Training

I trained three little girls to use the bathroom, and each experience was a completely different one. Since then, I have perfected the strategies used to the best of my ability in my classroom experiences. I am still learning and looking for consistent ways to help these little ones graduate to independence within their developmental time frames. At this juncture in my life, I have been teaching preschool special needs for seven years.

Previously, potty training was also necessary at the middle school and high school levels and was part of my repertoire of skills. It's a necessary life skill, and when not met, it must be worked on at any age. Even when there are medical conditions to consider, the routine of self-care skills should be addressed when appropriate. Many self- help skills are not only about the skill set but also about their dignity and independence, even at the emergent level. The heart of potty training with a young child, neurotypical or otherwise, is where they are at in their developmental stage. They really need to be ready. No tricks or coaxing will alter the child's ability before it's their time. They must understand what is being asked of them.

They physically should be able to interpret their body's signal. With children having medical considerations, the timelines can be completely different. Do not push them to make it happen before they are ready. Pushing before they're ready can contribute to unnecessary stress and anxiety for the child. Many variables exist when trying to understand what is happening with their bodies like sounds in the bathroom, flushing toilets, and timing.

It should be taught as a fun and natural event that we all participate in. With our babies on the spectrum, anxiety levels probably alter success most often, especially if all other areas mentioned have been satisfied. The child's absolute horror stemming from the flushing of the toilet to a continuum of flushing to the point of obsession is typical. It can be comical at times, and that's only the beginning. I can personally attest to numerous stories of plumbing disasters due mysterious items being flushed. I'll discuss the direction of potty training before plumbing issues for now. In order to train your child on the spectrum or those with other developmental delays, reinforcement is most usually needed. A pot of gold needs to be at the end of the rainbow, so to speak. Our children are not going to perform in any area for the sake of our desire, especially with bathroom skills.

Now, more of your investigative skills must come into play. What is your little one's favorite anything? Is it a computer or tablet? Is it a cupcake or a popsicle? Their favorites are your tricks of the trade. You must find the most unquenchable, desirable item that your child is willing to jump through hoops for and use it. I'm talking about the "top of the line" treat—the one that's not readily available *except* through the special opportunity of potty time. It cannot be any other way.

If your child has access to this most coveted item at any other time, it won't be as special, nor will it work as consistently.

For Bri, it was chocolate cupcakes—the horrible kind hidden in the pantry for a rainy day that you swear you never buy. She loved those sweet, hydrogenated, palm oil-laden chocolate cupcakes. Back then, I wasn't as organic as I try to be now, but that's another topic.

To train her, I took a picture of this forbidden delicacy and placed the picture on one side of an index card with a line drawn down the middle. The other side contained a picture of Bri's little potty chair. I showed her only the potty chair, had her label it "potty", clapping and cheering for the beautiful voice stating the obvious, and then we started the process. Next, I showed her only the picture of the cupcake. I described it as a yummy chocolate cupcake. Then I let the games begin.

I first introduced her to the toddler training potty chair and later moved to the cushiony Elmo training seat that sat on the regular toilet. I began with the direction of "Sit on the potty." She then ran all around the house, jumping on the furniture and giggling, and not be anywhere near the bathroom. I tracked her down and brought her back to the potty holding her little impish hand so she could try again. Round one, two, three for sure were hers to claim, but eventually she focused enough on the picture of the cupcake. I momentarily had her attention. Then, after whatever amount of time that took—days, weeks, months—once the actual activity took place and we had success, the celebration began. At the first attempt of achievement, we celebrated with cheering and singing, and the illustrious cupcake was given as the ultimate prize! Realize that this was only the first step. Consistency is key. I followed the same format for a duration until the activity became so ingrained and it belonged to her other skill sets. I cannot give you a timeline for it. Just be patient and enjoy the process. It is different for every child. The key is to use the most desired element in such a selective way to produce the outcome you want.

Now to tell you in reverse what potty training looked like for me with my neurotypical children, if there really is such a thing. My darling middle daughter was a baby herself just eight days shy of her second birthday when she was introduced to new baby sister, Bri. My precious Elana, my long-awaited-for second child, when it was her turn for potty training, she was still getting used to the novelty of a new sibling and had no interest. When I introduced the idea to her much later than I did with her older sister, she had absolutely no desire—Elana was not ready. The readiness of the child is the most important factor.

I had just brought home this tiny little alien into her kingdom. Everybody was fussing over this new pink bundle. There was the talk of tiny diapers and tiny feet, and naturally, she was not going to give up her position as the baby of our family without a fight. Our conversation went something like this, "I don't want to go potty. I like diapers." It was not a battle I chose at that time, for the mere reason that I had just given birth and was attempting to manage a family of three children for the first time. Choose your battles wisely, and choose your timing.

Now, my first daughter, Amanda, was a completely different scenario. Being a new mother at 24-years-old, she was like a little doll for me. One day, we walked into a bicycle store, and she spotted a tiny pink toddler bike. I didn't have seventy-five dollars for this bike, or I probably would have bought it on the spot, just because my little princess asked for it! I told my daughter that when she wore big girl pants, mommy would buy her that bike. That very day we went home, and she ran upstairs, took off her diaper, and put on big girl pants. I had been saving them to start practicing with Amanda. She went and sat on her potty chair. We had been practicing but not consistently at that point. Surprisingly, this child was not even two-years-old, yet that was the last day she wore diapers! In the next few days, I asked her grandmother to help me buy the little pink bike for her.

The power of reinforcement with all children is amazing! We all have our own currency. The trick is in finding the currency for your particular child in every situation. Readiness and reinforcement will get you started. Continue onward with consistency. I can now describe the over 40+ children who I have had success with during classroom experiences with potty training. The best strategies only worked at school when I had the support of their home environments as well.

Never forget that you are your child's first and best teacher and therapist. No professional can reach your child as well or as quickly as you can as their parent. I have been both at separate times in my life, and I have been both at the same time. The team you assemble for your child works because you are cooperating, giving of your insight, and helping with the process completely. The power is in the parenting! Your team only guides. In the classroom, I had the helpfulness of the group mentality. We sang songs about going potty. We watched Elmo go potty. We read social stories about going potty. The social pressure to be a big kid and the huge marketing push from the diaper industries makes learning how to go potty a superstar status! I use potty charts individualized with Thomas the Train, Dora, or whatever works best. Remember the search for the currency is the most vital. Using stars and stickers, I reinforced their efforts with the ability to earn up to five or six tickets in one clean sweep just for walking into the bathroom independently, approaching the toilet, pulling clothes down, and washing and drying hands. Look at how many steps are involved. It's no wonder it is a tedious task for our little ones.

In my classroom, I did my best to make going to the bathroom into one big party. The devil is in the details as far as reducing the anxiety level for our hyperarousal kiddos. In other words, if flushing is a big terror, then don't flush. Keep it simple. You are trying to get a little one with all kinds of sensory issues to filter out the scary and do what needs to be done. Any way that it can be accomplished is worth the investment.

Sometimes dim lighting or soft music can assist their comfort levels. Often, we ensured that the student was sufficiently hydrated to increase the chances of success. Individualize the reinforcement to make it worth their while. A good teacher tip is to call home when the child is successful at school. The joint effort works, and the immediate communication to parents makes their day as well as yours!

Praise, praise, praise their accomplishment. Praise and reinforce. Success means independence, and independence means moving on to the next step! I have touched on generalization and basic potty training. It is also important to touch on the sensory issues that are in direct relation to these strategies. If a skill, such as potty training is taught and remains somewhat consistent, it becomes a great foundation.

Unfortunately, there will be times when this skill disappears due to changes in environments, like a different bathroom during travel, or any other changes in the child's schedule. These times, however, can be opportunities for teaching the generalization of the skills taught at home or school. Other areas of jeopardy are when the body is relaxed and not attending to the bathroom protocol, such as when in the bathtub or a swimming pool.

When Bri was about two-years-old and her sister was four, there were unfortunately several incidences of surprises in the bathtub, which were extremely traumatizing to her sister and not in the least a problem for my sensory-seeking baby. She would just sweetly say, "Mama", and attempt to hand me her little gifts. It wasn't pretty, and created quite a loud bath time with the tears and yelling of her mortified sister! In hindsight, this was likely nothing more than a relaxed baby feeling no pressure to get out of the warmth of a bath to participate in her newly developed bathroom skills. Needless to say, the co-bathing ceased for a while. Thus, another lesson in generalization.

> *"Everything in the universe has a rhythm,*
> *everything dances." Maya Angelou*

14

Expect the Unexpected

With the case of any child, there will always be the unexpected happening that you, as a parent, could not have predicted. We caution our children not to touch things that are hot. We warn them not to put anything near an electrical outlet. We beg them not to climb too high or walk in front of a sibling on a swing. These standard dangers are passed down from generation to generation. Growing up in south Florida, we were always taught to swim at an early age because water is everywhere. I did the same for all of my children, especially Bri. Our main role as parents is to try to protect your children, all children, from dangers on a daily basis.

Somehow, our children on the spectrum can provide all of these concerns and more. They seem to look for the most creative ways to make alarms go off. Sometimes, it can occur in quite a literal way.

I can't tell you how many times as a teacher that I've heard the fire alarms go off in an elementary, middle, or high school setting. Usually, it happened when I was not with the student but not always. Once I was walking my class down to visit the Spanish class for special Cinco de Mayo celebration lunch. We had talked about walking quietly in the hallway. We practiced our greetings to friends and had discussions about not eating all of the food. I had practiced these concepts for about a week with this one particular class before our social gathering. We had visuals to prompt language, so we could share in the community setting. Down the hall we went, all six of us, four students with severe autism, my assistant, and myself. It was as if we were in slow motion, but I saw the fire alarm's red pull-down lever as big as life in front of me about two feet away. I tried to run ahead and cover it because it seemed to be calling the name of one of my female students. Before I could make it, her hands were on it, the alarm blared, and the doors in between the halls slammed shut!

I wished there was a rock for me to crawl under, because this malady was on me. Not that this student had a history of this behavior, because it was her first time, although it wasn't the last either. Soon we had a record of this repeated offense. For that time though, it was unexpected. Yet, I had to go straight to my principal's office and lay my head on the platter, so to speak. Going forward, it didn't happen on my watch, because I was vigilant with that particular student. It didn't mean that we wouldn't have copycat behaviors or a new student who needed to test out his skills.

With that one student, my team and I made signs that looked like fire alarms with a big X through them. We all took turns practicing with her. We took her to the visuals randomly placed around the school, which were paired with the actual fire alarm lever, and taught her the "Do not touch lesson" about three times a day for weeks, with the enduring stamina of my assistants with me. Then, we tested my prodigy by walking by about 10 alarms in the building, and as we approached the alarms, we pulled out the visual prompts. Standing far enough away from any potential disasters, we then asked her, "Do we touch? No touch. No touch red!" She giggled, but she didn't touch the alarms, not at least on our training walks.

That's not to say that over the four years that this child was my student, I didn't run back to my classroom every time the alarm went off in hopes that it wasn't her. There were at least three other times that it was. My specialized strategies had their limits for generalizing that behavior. I do want to mention that, with all of my experiences, practices, and strategies, in my classroom I had a remarkable team next to me. Just like when I emphasized your need for a support system in raising your child with a disability, a support system is equally important in the work environment. I cannot thank my coworkers enough for their hard work, creative ideas, and dedication to our students to make sure everyone was safe, learning and happy.

In the elementary school setting, I have had various surprises as well. There were numerous times that the little holes in the cafeteria chairs somehow enticed small little friends to stick their heads right through the hole. With my current class, whom I refer to as my "littles," I am constantly watching for new preschool tricks, and luckily their behavior has never caused us to make a call to the fire department. It's just that these things can happen in the blink of an eye, and they are mostly unpredictable.

I remember with my own daughter a situation where this was very true. It was a disastrous Saturday afternoon in which one of these most unforeseen events happened. Bri was sitting in her car seat, happily singing, as we were coming back from a long drive. She was playing with some measuring cups that had been in the car from   a classroom cooking project. It was all very harmless, except Bri loved to put her fingers into small objects. It was a sensory thing I'm sure, but I didn't know that much about sensory seeking at the time. I occasionally looked back in the rearview mirror to check on her. She was saying something, but she looked fine.

Then her little voice increased in volume, and I

assumed by mistake that she said one of her phrases that were just part of her echolalia. She repeated it louder and louder, "Stuck in, stuck in!". She also sounded more panicky. I reassured her that she was okay and not stuck in. Then it hit me like lightning. I looked at her face again, and she was stressed! I pulled the van over to the side of the street and walked to the back of the car. I found the absolute worst possible scene. She had her little baby finger stuck into the plastic handle of the measuring cup that she had been playing with. She was correct—she was stuck! She had been using what we refer to as borrowed language—a phrase from a television show or story to give meaning to what the child is trying to communicate. How I wished I had listened more intently a few minutes earlier. It was another opportunity to feel a tremendous amount of mother's guilt.

I scanned the situation with my daughter. I saw her little finger turning red and swelling inside this tiny cup's hole. The thought ran through my head: "Why did I let play with that?" I felt tortured, saying, "It's my fault! How do I get it off her finger?" Questioning myself to what I had in the car that could be used as a lubricant and finding nothing, I searched in a frenzy. Sheer panic set in as I drove a little faster to a fire station, only to find it isolated.

I jumped back in the car with Bri stressing and the cup still on her finger. The swelling continued. I ran into a drug store, where the pharmacists hearing the fear in my voice offered some slippery liquid, one after the other, and nothing worked. Bri began to cry. I began to cry. I got back in the car, and flew down the highway to Children's Healthcare of Atlanta, the best hospital for children in general and in special situations. I don't remember how I parked the car or if I even parked it, it was all a blur. I took Bri into the emergency entrance and was greeted by a band of angels. I speak quickly on a typical day, but that day I am sure gibberish came out of my mouth. I tried to give the facts. I explained the measuring cup on her finger. I explained autism. I explained that I am so sorry that I had measuring cups in my car for her to play with.

They took her into a room, brought out a special ring-cutting scissor, and she was saved. It took them seconds to save the day. Thank God! Thanks to the talented doctors and nurses that know what to do in a panic. It took months to get over the feeling of being an idiot as a parent. It was unforeseen and unpredictable, and I wish I could have handled it better. I know we all feel this as parents, from time to time, but during times like that, it seems to cut so much deeper for those of us with special children.

The need to protect a child that cannot fend for herself is so huge. It is a sense of needing to shelter them from all harm, and that as a parent of any child is an impossible feat. So, we move on, looking for the next unpredictable event to be a little more predictable.

With that situation behind me, I realize that I am quite blessed that my child hasn't gotten into more precarious situations than she has. She's lucky to not have had more serious injuries, especially the way she always sought out small or tight places to squeeze her body into for sensory satisfaction. She always surprised me with the way she played. I spent the good part of 10 years outside, exploring every park between Georgia and Florida. It all depended on where we were at that time, as I was always desperately trying to entertain three children. A park always seemed like a good choice for the whole lot. Bri loved the swing, although at times she was way past the age and size of the toddler swing. She would climb up and before I knew what had happened, she was trying to get into it. She insisted on attempting to halfway smash her fat little toddler legs halfway through the swing holes before I could retrieve her. The insistence of bigger body parts into smaller places became a recurring nightmare. She also backed up into the under part of the slide to just feel the squeeze of her wiggly body forced still between the stiff warm plastic. On the other hand, she also slid the fireman pole at the park at two-years-old and performed as if she were five! My middle daughter, Elana, who was two years older wouldn't even attempt that. She had a better sense of danger and limitations. Bri was never fearful, which meant I was always watching over her like a hawk.

I wish I knew then what I know now about sensory needs and regulation. It's what drove me to write this book. I want to share with you the combination of what I didn't know, how I survived, and what I learned. I want to reveal the new understanding of what I know now. It is a constant learning experience. I always tell people two things about raising Bri. One, that with all that I learned in graduate school with a second degree in special education, I learned far more by being Bri's mother. Secondly, my other two children that I have and love were much more complicated and difficult to raise than Bri. I say this to them all the time with love and laughter but a lot of truth as well.

There is a rhythm to raising a child with autism. Once you walked through the desert of darkness, once you face the monsters, accept that this is your path and your child's path. They need us so desperately to hold their hand, to be their voice, and to be the Warrior Mom or Dad to fight the battles that they are not even aware exist. This is the price. It's not small, but it is worth it. With every therapy you take part in, every book you read, and every parent you share your pain with, you receive hope, and you give hope. It is a very beautiful doable life. You just need a few tricks up your sleeve to make it easier for everybody.

"All great achievements require time." Maya Angelou

15

Foundations of Safety and Independence

When Bri would run free as the wind, I would panic. I couldn't lose her. She was so unnaturally quick for a child her age. I would chase her, and like any child, she would love it. So, with running, that was our rhythm. When her little body showed me that it was time to be set free, I took her out of the stroller and let her be. When she stopped to look at me, I would chase her. It was our beautiful dance. All children love this game. I can attest to that, as I am still doing it daily with my current preschoolers. Some of my students have autism, and some have other disabilities, but they all want to play chase and run.

The difference is, with children on the spectrum, the connection is in that "stop and look at mom" moment. In that split second of time, they are saying, "I'm here, are you?" It's your chance to play but also to get that connecting response. That social engagement from your little one is so important. Sometimes it comes with language but not necessarily. It's the invisible cord between a parent and child or a teacher and student. You must make something big of it. Teachers, this counts for you as well, as it must be taught precisely. You must teach it, reinforce it, and then maintain the contact early on and forever. Let me explain. One of the most important targets we teach is to have a child respond to their name. Sounds easy enough, but with our children it can be very difficult, and we have no choice!

To have our children recognize their own name and respond when called is the basis for all safety with them. It has to be driven into their little brains that each and every time you call out to your child, they are to look and respond. It comes first before other safety measures. If taught consistently and their response is consistent, when in danger, you can call out and you'll get their attention.

With Bri, I sang songs about her beautiful name and

made up silly rhymes. I used verbal play with her constantly. "Where's Bri?" I played with her. I said her name and then my name, and so on. Each parent has their own way, but the important part is to get that concept well-formulated in their head. To be sure it works, as pertaining to safety, I also practiced all the time when it wasn't an urgent situation, taking consideration not to overdue the strategy to make it ineffective. If she were playing, I called her name relatively close to her, then call her name again and waited if I received no response, which happened quite a lot in the beginning. Receiving no response is the reason that hearing is usually the first step in evaluating our kids, as any hearing loss must be ruled out first. They do present in the beginning as if they cannot hear. This, however, was not the case with Bri. She could hear. She was tuning me out, so I would scoop her up and call her name, telling her "Your name is Brianna." Bri is her nickname. I would say her full name over and over in verbal play.

Continue this play until it works. It may sound

redundant, and it may appear that our children are not focused or even intelligent enough to get the game. However, the opposite is true. They simply are tuning into the channel they like best. They have superpowers for tuning out what they are not impressed with. So, guess what? You, as the parent, must crank it up! You need to get their attention for this and other strategies, but most importantly get their attention for this one. It will come, trust me. It's difficult but important parent work. The one time that you need to call your child to protect them, you'll be thankful that their response is consistent, and that they respond to your urgency. I've had many runners in my career and in my life, including my own daughter. This skill set kept them safe. Even if they take off, and they will, when you call their name and they respond by looking and stopping, you will be able to keep them safe. Sometimes a matter of seconds counts.

With more severe cases and more intense runners, you have to change the game to be more reinforcing than the chase or escape. In the classroom environment, I produced positive results with this type of situation by always having a pocket full of something fabulous like fruit gummies. When the child ran, I called their name. I kept in close proximity and just stopped them for a second. When they stop, praise them for looking and for stopping. Give them the treat as the reinforcement. You need to keep this momentum in order to teach the skills you want to see throughout the day.

The rhythm of autism is a flow between verbal and nonverbal communication. Before our kids are communicating verbally, they are watching and listening. There is no doubt about this. Every child that has crossed my path, including children with the most severe autism, understood so much more than they let on. Maybe it feels safer for them to stay in their little cocoon. It's our place, however, to prove that to be wrong.

Earlier, I mentioned how Bri understood so much but was only verbalizing up to five words. This didn't improve until well after her third birthday. It was torture waiting for her language to come. However, she was right in line with understanding my requests. If I asked her to bring me something, she would on the first request. Now to be fair, I was working very hard on increasing her receptive vocabulary. I labeled everything and everyone at all times. I constantly asked her, "Who is that?" I asked her, "What is that?", responding with, "It's a ball. A big ball." You get the picture. You always go back to the basics for language acquisition. By doing that, you feed their language part of the brain with the information they need. When asked to follow a direction to go get their shoes or something, they'll then recall the vocabulary that you've been teaching them by showing them the object, person, or place, and then giving it the name to learn and recall. Do this with every item or person in their environment. Do it around the clock. Teach it, and reteach it, until it is generalized.

Expressive language is so much more difficult to learn, and it will take more time. In the meantime, our children are taking it all in. If I asked Bri to bring me something, it was to produce this back-and-forth flow rhythm. Our children build relationships with us, and at the same time, they connect with the object they are pursuing. "Bring me the ball" is a request that demands listening, following directions, responding to your voice, and making a connection. This is true of every request and every opportunity of labeling objects. This is the rhythm. You must learn to listen to it and make it happen with every strategy that you implement.

This flow between parent and child can be with a look or a touch. It is the communication as well as a safety net for our kids. They are so trapped in their bodies that cannot perform what they know inside. We are just beginning to learn in the autism field how true this is. Hopefully, someday we'll find communication therapies that produce promise for our children. There are children with autism who, upon finding their voice, tell therapists and families what we all have always known. They are complete in their thoughts, ideas, and humanity. They simply don't have the organization of thought, nor the ability to express it. It doesn't make it non-existent, however. Our job is to pull it out of them, which isn't very easy especially at first, but over time it will come. Praise them with clapping and sing songs for every look or response they provide. It's the most important area to reinforce. As a parent, you'll also need this type of connection. Their responses will be few and far between in the beginning. With some kids, it will look like there's not a connection. Yet, there is a connection—there is always a connection, no matter how minute.

If you're a parent of a child with autism, you already know how sweet and affectionate they can be. How unfortunate for the mothers decades ago who were labeled "refrigerator moms" and blamed for being cold-hearted because their child didn't show a typical response. This horrible injustice to those families at that time was tragic. Now, what is known is that some children are hypersensitive due to sensory deficits. They may react to touch, fabric, or sound in a vulnerable way, so that at first, they reject their environment. They are not, however, rejecting their parent. All children respond to positive surroundings that include sounds, softness, and especially touch, which is essential to the growth and development of all children, including babies in the animal kingdom. The need to touch and be touched is life.

Babies that cry and are soothed until they feel better to have much less anxiety. To help a child learn to self-soothe is also important for when you are not available. However, in the first couple of years and beyond, it's vital to show children love with physical affection and play. Studies now show that physical affection actually affects brain development. So, hold, hug, and play with them, even when there is tactile defensiveness. It's necessary.

Some of my sweetest moments with Bri were the times that we shared that connection. At this point in our lives, I can elicit a response from her on demand at any time, but that wasn't always the case. She was so fast and in constant motion. It was difficult to get her to be still for the slightest moment. When I picked her up, I would look directly into her eyes and speak with her. She looked everywhere around her, wanting to get down, like any energetic toddler but more intense. It was almost like a fight or flight response and not just a simple desire to explore. I would continue to get her attention by jumping up and down with her, and then I would stop. I'd look at her and say "Hi" as enthusiastically and dramatic as I could. With direct eye contact, I then asked, "What do you want?" "More?" I would suggest. She then would use some basic sign language and eventually began to verbalize an approximation of the word, "more." I followed up by jumping more.

I am sure you recognize the pattern now. Whether it's language, activity, or eye contact, we as parents or therapists must be the reinforcement. My favorite line from an influential doctor and applied behavioral analyst was that we have to be the big M&M! In other words, it has to be worth their while to perform. The currency of our children might be action, food, or any number of things.

I continued with Bri to always try to make talking with mommy fun or at least rewarded her with jumping or something that was fun for her. These little connections continued throughout her baby years because I worked at it until it was natural. You'll find your rhythm with your own child and recognize the connections for your own family. Note, it can also look different at various stages of their development.

When Bri was school-aged, especially at the middle school stage, she would be exhausted at the end of the day. She used to sit behind the driver's seat in my van. I would put my hand back to request her hand and she would hold my hand. I learned how to tell by the way she presented her hand what kind of day she was having. If it were fast and furious, or if she kept holding mine, it translated into what kind of day she had or how she was currently feeling.
This connection helped both of us.

Each child is different, and each parent is different in their style of communicating with their offspring. This is more about strategies to elicit a response. Even if you are a quieter or introverted parent, you will find ways to command this connection with your child. The main point is to be consistent. If you are trying to get eye contact or a verbal response, keep trying and be flexible. If one way is not working, try another. Some new brain studies show that it may not be a best practice to demand eye contact due to the fact that it may be very aversive to do so with some children on the spectrum. Eye contact is something we use to make sure someone is listening. Yet, for our children, it may present some physical difficulty to do so and is something to pay attention to. If your child seems to be really opposed to direct eye contact, try something else. A great many of our children on the spectrum enjoy deep pressure, craniosacral therapy, or massage, which can also be a way of providing the connection between you and your child. Bri always wanted and still wants for her sisters or myself to "squish" her. She wants to press your face into hers at almost a painful pressure. Sometimes, she now asks for "tickle pressure" because she is craving the deep pressure in her joints or spine. This is more than a deep pressure at our house.

It enabled her to request the connection of her siblings to play with her.

"When we do the best that we can, we never know what miracle is wrought in our life, or in the life of another." Helen Keller

16

Joint Attention

Later in their development as children with autism start to see their parents as a person who can navigate their world for them, they will start to use joint attention. According to Wikipedia, "Joint attention or shared attention is the shared focus of two individuals on an object by means of eye-gazing, pointing or other verbal or non- verbal indications."

I explain joint attention using this example: When a parent points to an airplane in the sky and says "airplane," a typical child responds back, repeating the word "airplane" with a finger in the air. This skill sometimes takes a lot of work to teach to our children on the spectrum. Some of our kids develop this skill naturally, but most of the time it must be taught directly. Many of my students, as well as my daughter, used my arm or hand to pick something off of the floor, instead of just picking it up themselves. They actually prefer to use our body parts to get what they need, like the pushing a parent's elbow to hand them a glass from which to drink. All of these are examples of joint attention. My favorite story of joint attention with my Bri is an example of waiting a long time to see how she really understood what I was trying to say to her. When she was about two-years-old, I took her outside and pointed to the moon. Every night, I did this with her. For years, I would raise my arm and raise her little hand, and say, "Look at the moon." She didn't seem to pay much attention to me or the moon. Then one day, years later, we were swimming at a friend's subdivision on a summer night. Night was falling, and Bri, who swam like a fish, was swimming back and forth. She swam up to me, got in my arms, and pointed to the sky, using my arm to point as well, as said," Mama, look at the moon!" I cried uncontrollably in the water with my friends. I was so relieved that she had been listening to all of those years. My words, my efforts, had not been in vain. My baby girl had been paying attention the whole time over the course of several years! It simply wasn't her time to give it back to me until that night. It is the sweetest of memories, and it was a night of a valuable lesson. This moment confirmed to me that the work that we put into our children is never wasted energy. It all comes together at some point, although it may look different with each child. As a parent, I felt like I had to do something, but at that time I didn't feel like I did anything more than I did for my other children. I sang to all three of my children from the womb. I read them the classics— the stories that all children learn. I nursed all of them. I followed the pediatrician's advice on when to start solid food. I bought the toys and played outside, likely more with the last two, because I bought a big outdoor swing set with a picnic table and all the extras. We had a little more money than with our first child when we were so young. Resources provided for a little more with the addition of two more children, and it was a great excuse to buy the fancy playset.

The point is that good parenting and enjoying the development of your child, any child, is the same in the framework. The things that may make me look back and wonder whether I did enough for Bri are most likely ramifications of more unnecessary guilt. Do what comes naturally to you in your parenting. Expect good behavior when you teach the appropriate behavior. If your typical child didn't climb on furniture, don't let your child on the spectrum do it. Work on language with your every breath until you have some communication with your child on any level. Raise your baby. Teach your baby. Granted the repetitions to master a skill may be a thousand times more than another child of yours. Be patient.

Research shows that with kids on the spectrum, skills such as reading take a lot more man hours to teach than with typical child. Repetition is the key. The patterns in the story, the vocabulary, and the relationship to the characters all are built stronger with more reading. Even reading the same story repeatedly is extremely beneficial. Maybe, if I knew then what I know now when Bri was tiny, I would have read *The Three Little Bears* 50 times, instead of 30. There's no exact science, but it's essential to follow the clues that your child gives you of his or her interest in reading or any other area of learning. Our children work best and learn best when they're interested in the subject, so we should use it to our advantage. If your child is obsessed with the solar system, then read every book you can on it. If the story of the three bears is popular with your child, try and read 20 more books about bears. This type of grouping helps with the generalization of language concepts.

Whatever childhood development concepts are good for typical kids, then they are good for our kids as well. Read the stories, build the blocks, get out the modeling clay, paint, and enjoy! Keep trying new things, and keep following your instincts as a parent with your child.

"I am only one, but still I am one. I cannot do everything, but still I can do something; And because I cannot do everything I will not refuse to do the something that I can do." Helen Keller

17

Take the Lead

Our children's deficit areas like communication and social skill development demand us as parents to take the lead role. It's within the process of building relationships with our children that we start to see the connections so necessary for their growth.

As previously mentioned, joint attention is the basis for this communication and relationship building. If your child uses your hand to reach a cup, this shared effort is connecting you with your child. You become the connector to the outside world, as well as the mediator between your child and the object of his or her desire. You must build on this constantly. It's not that you become the only way that they can function by reaching something that they need. Instead, you are participating in their world. The tiniest look from your child to you and vice versa is a lifeline to keeping them connected and pulling them into a bigger world. In a

10-minute interaction, this connection could look something like the following. A look exchanged from your child to you, and then a gaze at the bowl in the cabinet—this connection opens up a communication opportunity. You might know exactly what it means. It could mean that a bowl is used for ice cream, and your child has a craving for ice cream. You need to act like you have no idea what it means. You have to almost sabotage the environment in attempts to draw out more connection and more language from your child. Some kids can become quite creative to avoid these connections. I have seen many littles including my own, go and get a big chair to gain access to what they want, instead of putting forth the effort to communicate with me.

Remember, the nature of autism is to be alone, find their own interests, and keep their world small and safe. We have to change and shift those patterns with all that we have. Leave no stone unturned in this process. Without looking back to test my own skills as a parent of a child with special needs, I am constantly learning and adapting to her needs, but there are a few things I know for sure. With every big hug, every up-in-the-air-with-laughter moment, and every showering of kisses counted, she was the audience for my biggest show, and I had to work hard to entertain her and keep her attention. In getting and keeping her attention, I was able to make the minimal demands for language and reciprocal behaviors that put her in our world and not lost in isolation. There were days when I watched her line up her little counting bears for the longest time. It was sweet to watch her interact in her pretend world, putting the bears in a circle of friends, and being happy. I gave her some time for her fantasy, and then I interfered.by counting the bears with her, and then asking how many bears were there and what colors were there. She would've been happy enough to be left alone, and I would've been happy enough to let her peacefully play. Yet, I could not—it wasn't enough for her. I had to lure her into a little bit of mommy time. I had to do that with every opportunity. Luckily, you'll get creative after a while, and it will become less work.

Clapping hands together, singing songs, any cause and effect are all ways to make those early connections. Sometimes a snuggle replaces eye contact. All contact that is reciprocal in some way is a good contact. It is so special and rewarding when you get that sideways glimpse. It's almost visible at times, like a tiny lightning strike—that moment when you are completely in sync with your child—nothing matters more. I can tell you that the beautiful thing in my life is the constant growth of that connection with Bri. It looks much different now because she is 18. The work I put into building that relationship is apparent now, but it wasn't back when she was small. Then, it was only a matter of a mother's instinct wanting her baby to be loved and happy.

Every time I've seen her eyes look directly into mine has been a gift. Even now, when I pick her up from school and she recognizes my car and comes to me independently, and before the headphones and the sunglasses enable her to tune me out like any other teenager, she gives me the glance. The look that if she could spontaneously say "Hi, Mom, I had fun at school today." or something to that effect possibly. We learn to read through the lines and the communication, however, silent at times but still evident. When she was younger, it was amazing to me each time she responded to a request with a look, or by just coming close to me, or even jumping right on me. That was always the best. It was the connection that said," I am here, right with you." It often takes work, and it takes seeing what is really happening and not just feeling like it is a coincidence. This is the beautiful bond that you have to create with your child and for your child. It's also essential to enable them to make other relationships with other people in their future and in all environments. It begins with you. It's easy if you think of it as falling in love every day with this precious creature, and bringing them along on an amazing journey. Making this connection is a true labor of love that benefits everyone in your family and in your child's world.

To the teacher reading this book, this counts for you as

well. I have been blessed in my 30-year career to build connections with quiet little souls who are hiding in corners, playing with tape on the wall. In time, they became my shadow. It took work, creativity, flexibility, and many ideas to be thrown out the window, only to start again the next day, and try something new. It's a puzzle. We have the privilege to get to know so many little strangers and make them our little friends. Take the challenge seriously, do the work, and enjoy the journey.

"If I cannot do great things, I can do small things in a great way." Dr. Martin Luther King Jr.

18

Building Bridges

The relationships we build begin with us for our children. However, they also need to expand their relationships to include others pretty early on. For the obvious reasons, we want our children to feel comfortable with other family members, peers, and other important people in their life. Depending on the birth order of your child with autism or other disabilities, this may look different. In my case, with Bri being my third child and my youngest, it was somewhat dictated to me. I had the natural environment of an older sibling 11 years older and two years older than Bri. The environment provided opportunities for language and social models, in addition to survival with two other sisters. This is for all families.

Research shows how sibling positions in families orchestrate personality development, social skills, and interpersonal skills. Evidence even suggests that based on your own position in the family, you might be better married to an opposite personality for better relations.

Being the oldest in my family definitely influenced how I see the world. Having siblings around can also be very helpful for the younger child to be interested in what the family is doing. It provides room for great practice with language imitation. With Bri being in the baby position, my other children constantly reminded me how everything was for the baby over them. I'm hoping their interpretation is skewed, but either way it made me laugh. Yes, Bri was the baby, who happened to be born with autism. I am sure there are many truths to both sides. Obviously, the child with special needs demanded more of my attention, but I agree with the girls that there was a definite baby factor going on. The lovely thing about our family is that I can testify with all my heart that, although our path was not planned, it influenced my older girls in such positive ways of who they became as human beings. I am sure they would've grown up to be the caring, nurturing individuals that they are. Bri just added an element of fierceness to their sisterhood. They watched over her, defended her, and protected her their entire young lives. In the early years, it wasn't so lovely and not so planned. As I mentioned earlier, while jumping in with both feet to new therapies with Bri, I had a three-year-old along with us. She still reminds me to this day of how torturous it was to watch through the black glass while Bri had "fun." I couldn't help it. The therapy sessions had to be done. I would've done it for any of my kids, but that's not what mattered to a toddler.

It also doesn't forgive my nearsightedness with her. Time was crunched. I was working. I was also terrified at the prospect of what this autism label meant for my little one. I was teaching full time with middle schoolers with the most severe and aggressive forms of autism. I was drowning. Scheduling was difficult for after-school therapy, but it was the only way I could keep my job. If I apologized to my little girl a million times over, it would never be enough. I can't change history, and to tell you the truth, if in the same position, I'm not sure how I would've done it differently. I advise you, if you're struggling with a similar predicament, go back to your village. Find your people who can help. Your team of warriors is ready to assist with your schedule. Ask for assistance and get the family   and babysitter involved! I tried, did it all by myself, and that was a mistake. It affected everyone and only left me feeling guilt-ridden and exhausted.

For my daughter that patiently waited in the observation room while her little sister learned to speak, you are my heart and my hero. Bri could not have had a better set of sisters. She is lucky for it, and so am I. As far as my oldest, she was also the biggest help growing up with her sister. My oldest, Amanda, operated at 11-years-old as a second mommy. She was that and more for both of her sisters. One of the joys of having children when you're young is that basically you grow up together. Amanda was always my best little friend and such an amazing part of Bri's language and social development. The relationship building that took place in our home between siblings was always something to behold with never a dull moment. My oldest was so charming with her tiniest audience. There were violin concerts just for Bri with her favorite, "Twinkle, Twinkle Little Star". There were songs made up just for Bri's entertainment. Elana was so little, but she would teach her sister the ins and outs of baby life. She occasionally offered Bri a toy just to take it away from her. I didn't say it was perfect, but it was very normal. With short of two years between the babies, there was a constant back and forth of whether or not Elana wanted to keep the new baby or return her to the hospital from whence she came.

Through the expanding family life, Bri found her place. Relationships developed daily with her sisters. She was part of a group, which is a very important concept for our kids to participate in. It makes learning their environment much more fluid because they have to keep up with the flow of the family. If everyone is piling into the van, then Bri was less anxious and went along with her sisters. If they played outside, she also played.

All children learn from each other so much faster than any adults. This was so true for Bri.

If her sisters were making bubble noises with their mouths, she attempted to the same. If they repeated a word or sang a song, Bri participated at her level. I recall one amazing vacation trip coming home from Florida where I heard the most complicated tongue-twister of a song coming from an angelic voice. I looked in the rearview mirror, only to see Bri singing! I was totally convinced that it was Elana, my middle daughter, but no, it was the baby! I asked enthusiastically who had taught her that song. Both of my daughters laughed like I was crazy. I was overjoyed in the understanding. The sisters taught her so much, good and bad through those years. It was an important lesson for me to see how motivation played such a key role in her imitation. To keep up with the big sisters was the highest motivation, and it worked over and over again. It still works to this day, even though her sisters have adult lives now. Bri still gets so excited to see them every chance she gets.

Sibling relationships are also is something that should be monitored and developed. In the case of my own family, there were hurt feelings and imbalance as far as real-mommy time and perceived- mommy time. Either way, all the children need time and validation and enough attention from their parents. I didn't win this battle, but I'm trying to do better as the girls have grown and their needs are changing, which is difficult. The squeaky wheel, as the saying goes, changes from time to time. You oil where you need to. I have also seen in my career experiences where the sibling relationships were great, and other times where they were quite strained for various reasons. The nature of the beast is that the parent is kidnapped to the world of doctors, therapists, and evaluations. It cannot be altered. Money plays a role, resources like insurance plays a role, and the family plays a role. I've seen in some families where the typical child becomes the super achiever in the family, attempting to make up for their sibling's weaknesses and make the family whole again. I have witnessed the angry sibling that wreaks havoc on the family through behaviors of their own to try and gain some of the attention they so desperately need. Finally, there's the passive sibling who does everything for the child in need, forsaking their own identity. A thousand combinations exist of who and what the typical sibling comes to be within this family dynamic. Hopefully, with careful consideration, all children can get what they need from the family and come out better for it.

Other family relationships are also willing or unwilling partners in this adventure. There are grandparents, aunts, and uncles, even friends who can assist in helping to create this atmosphere of balance and love. It's so much more complex than everyone joyfully celebrating this new child with a few problems here and there. First of all, you must deal with the acceptance or denial of whether or not something is different from the development of the child. You'll hear so many excuses or ideas, which are well-intended but never the less more opinions than one family needs. It takes a while for most families to come to a consensus about what the plan is. The considerations for medical care, educational training, and therapeutic decisions can all be up for discussion in an open-minded family, or there's reality.

In our family, the reality was that everyone told me things about Bri that I could not see, nor did I want to. I said before I wasn't ready to admit to any of her disability, and was ready to fight anyone who said anything differently. Once past that denial, the picture became clearer to me. Babies are babies, and it's no different for our children on the spectrum.

Grandparents hold, spoil, and enjoy their grandchildren, which is how it should be. Having family to confide in and express your own feelings of inadequacy as well in this process, and again being able to ask for help is essential. It won't be smooth at all time, I can guarantee that.

As a parent, you'll be protective over your child and believe that only you can understand the kaleidoscope of feelings you're having. Your instincts are exaggerated with a child who cannot speak in the typical time frame.

You are guarding that child like a mother or father lion. You are on a mad search to find the right doctor, therapist, or a new treatment that is going to save your child. You don't sleep without dreaming about your child and his or her needs—it's endless. I can tell you it has been like that for my last 18 years. They stay on your mind at all times, which is why it's so important to develop the family connections who give you a break. Your child also needs to know that other people in the family and extended family are also be a safe refuge for them. In my own family and extended family, there were offers of prayer, sympathy, and sometimes money. All of these were acts of love for Bri. My husband worked around the clock to ensure that she was financially taken care of, as well as the rest of the family. This was all a part of our family dynamics. Everyone was offering their best. I needed more, but I didn't know it at the time, most likely because I was a special education teacher and supposed to know what I was doing. I took on the bigger battles by myself, with my other two children at my side. It's why I suggest taking a look at the big picture for everyone's best interest. For this reason, I implore you to ask for all the help you can get. Just like with any child, there are times in your life that you simply need a break. Needing it and taking it are two different things when you don't have a support system in place.

Work on your base and gather up support for yourself and your child through family or college students looking to learn about special education or with similar interests. Choose anyone that you feel will supervise effectively and give you the time you need. Our job as parents of young children with autism can be tricky at best. To be honest, part of the reason I didn't leave Bri with anyone except occasionally with family was because it was so much work to prepare to be gone. I felt like I almost paid for it twice because some crazy shenanigans would take place in my absence. For example, it could've been just a really messy kitchen because I had left the kids in charge, or coming home to Bri having set out all my fine china to throw a tea party for all of her stuffed animals. Either way, I learned that a messy kitchen can be cleaned up, and time to get your mental health in order is more important. Some of the tricks that I employed was to stage the play area or table full of fun things for her to do that were not the usual. It made my absence less dramatic and gave her something new to explore. During this time when Bri was younger, I bought interesting little cups to hold her crayons or very large paper for her to draw with on an easel or just anything new. Presenting old toys in new ways kept her interest and enabled her to explore independently with art supplies or toys. Expanding her interests or showing her new things also helped to generalize previous skills and really keep her occupied for longer time periods for those times at home or out of the house when I needed a little mom time. Our children love to open little containers, check out the contents, and put it all back together. Take caution with littles that are prone to put small objects in various orifices. A few new bottles or plastic items will entertain them and help with fine motor skills. Finding tiny things to put in them or coins to push through slots on piggy banks are also good ways to keep the busy little hands learning and exploring.

I used to look for the seasonal sales at stores for funny piggy banks in the shape of sharks or surfing pigs. Bri loved those plastic coin holders. I would place all of my change in front of her, and she stayed busy. As our children get older, you can use the coins also as language opportunity for labeling the coins and comparing the size of them. Use every opportunity to teach multi-layers of skills. Always remember that our children with autism are intelligent in their own ways, and filling them with new information in a natural environment is always beneficial. Bri still likes to put money into containers to this day, although now she has figured out the purchasing power of the almighty dollar, as well as a credit card.

Some things are universal in how they pick up on what will get them the things they want. For example, any old puzzle pieces or parts from old games can be repurposed for different games or ways to explore, label, and play. Another item that can keep them busy as well as understanding new concepts is plain old chart paper taped on the wall. We know, especially when they are little, that the vertical position of using an up-and-downward direction of their little arms such as when painting helps to strengthen their muscles. It's like they are exercising and painting at the same time. Good motor work promotes calming behavior and language development, as well as simply enjoying the activity. With Bri at home, if I used a template for her to color or paint within, it was large. (I also use this template in my classroom.) I place a large outline of a bear, or just plain paper, and allow the children to tell me what they painted. It reiterates the point of so many levels necessary to teach, and it all can be done in a five- to ten-minute session with the right materials, time, and space that the child needs.

Many of our little ones on the spectrum can have tactile defensiveness. Meaning, they don't want to touch anything they don't like. Shaving cream, paint, crayons, anything can trigger a defensive approach to working with these materials. In addition, it can be caused by strong odors, the feel of the product, or any other number of sensory factors. In my preschool Special Needs classroom as well as with Bri, it doesn't mean you stop exposing them to new items. What you do is provide exposure in small doses, and place items out on the table or easel at their level. Allow them to explore in their own time. If their time is never, you'll want to get creative on how to get them to just try it a little, even if it will trigger a negative response. If a total meltdown occurs, it may just be bad timing and/or seem overwhelming at the time, so you can stop. Just be sure to try again later, like in a few days to give them another opportunity to try new things. Always allow them as many experiences with new things to attempt. What else do you need to make a sensory paradise for your little ones with autism? The world is at your hand nowadays, with Pinterest and craft stores galore, but how do know what to put into a sensory bin? Luckily, many fabulous websites now understand our basic vocabulary of sensory stimulatory and calming environments. You don't need anything fancy to begin with, so don't worry about running out and spending lots of money. You probably have the basics around the house. I used beans in a sand and water table. Be aware, though, that beans sprout. But that's okay if that happens because then you have an automatic garden activity. Water, rice, beans, pasta, and sand are all great sensory tools to place in your small or large buckets. Kids need to feel the different textures run through their hands for sensory input, which is true for the good development of all children. All kinds of cups, bowls, spoons, and other utensils can be used to help with sensory as well as pretend play. I like the kinetic sand products that are available for molding. The sand doesn't stick to their hands, so it helps with our littles who are tactile defensive.

Remember, all activities should be combined with language. If your child is enjoying running through the beans with his hands, grab a handful and count with them. Hold them up to your face and pretend they are your eyes or nose. Playful language and modeling are always beneficial and will expand your play session.

Water is also popular for pouring, measuring, and sensory exploration. I love to buy the sand toys at the end of a season from some of the big-box stores and use them in the water table. Some real learning takes place as children watch the water flowing through windmills or funnels. Another way to expand on the play with water is to   use toys like plastic fish or sea creatures that they have to scoop   up with their hands or a fishing rod. I sometimes go to the bigger hardware stores and get small wooden toggles to make into fishing rods. You can put magnets on a plastic fish, tie a string on the rod, and go fishing! You can also practice labeling the colors or names of the sea friends. This learning play can be hours of entertainment and sensory satisfaction, as well as language development. In my classroom where time is a premium, I have the students help me in the process of building or making something like the fishing rod, if possible. We measure the string, practice with the magnets before assembly, and when the project is complete in a few minutes, they have participated in the creation of the final product. Then, we play.

Enjoying these moments with your child also helps normalize play from therapy sessions. It's therapeutic as well, but you can also enjoy just regular time with your child while creating fun memories. You're always changing their neural pathways while at play and with incidental teaching, but sometimes it's just about the fun! Another great hands-on activity is gardening. Do a little research for what seasonally grows in your area. You want to look for quick- growing plants or vegetables. Using something that illustrates an immediate cause and effect, especially with little ones, will help develop the understanding of gardening. Our children don't have a natural wait time, so the faster growing like beans, the better. Little children love to play in the dirt. Some of our kids won't at first, but start small. Wearing garden gloves and using small paper cups and plastic gardening tools can be less intimidating sensory wise to some of our less enthusiastic gardeners. In my classroom, we planted in the classroom, and then replanted in the garden. By the end of the semester, the preschoolers could tell or show you all of the steps with planting.

"The seeds, water, and sunshine help the plants grow" was our visual and verbal mantra daily. They would show anyone willing to listen what we were growing—radishes, lettuce, and carrots. As a class, we even attempted a taste-testing party with our vegetables. Some children were true tasters because they had taken part in the entire process and were highly invested. You can grow a garden on a smaller scale right in your own backyard. The experience is so worth it!

No matter what your materials are at hand, old toys, small objects, or organic material, just get busy with your child and explore. Watch their interests and language grow. Along with setting up play areas for sensory needs, these other environments can also be a place to address their deficits.

Sensory needs are so complex and different with each child and at different times. Some of our kids will request the extra squeezes or touches through words or body language. Some will need you to take the lead with brushing protocols or soft touches with varying materials. It's part of your child's sensory diet and is best initiated with your occupational therapist. You can still follow your child's lead, however, with the communication they provide you in this area.

Our children still need downtime and unstructured play to explore and find their interests. Allow for it daily and at several intervals. Use it as this time to you watch and listen to how they are seeing their world, and then you can participate on their level of play. It is a constant balancing act of letting them show us, and then we show them. For them, much joy can be had in the lining up of small cars or toys. The order and the patterns they choose is their way to show us their thinking. It is okay. It's actually good and beautiful, and it not only should be allowed at times but praised. Their brains work differently, and they are still intelligent children with their own ideas. They have much to learn to participate in our world, and we must take advantage of those teaching moments and fill them with knowledge. But remember, they are still little and need to have it their way some of their day, as well.

"It always seems impossible until it's done."

Nelson Mandela

19

Sensory and Sleep

With Bri, it was always blatantly obvious that she was the most sensory-seeking child on the planet. A slight exaggeration maybe, but trust me, she's a close second to any other little astronaut flying into orbit at a constant rate. From her earliest walking, she was on the move. If she climbed one stair, she could (and did) climb everyone one of them. She would walk up the stairs, carrying a gallon of milk or five Elmo's, but they didn't slow her down. She was a naturally a cuddly infant. She was very easy to hold with never a complaint. She didn't require a lot of cuddles, but I couldn't resist. She was easily self-soothed with a pacifier, and laid in her bassinet and crib with no resistance every time. She received plenty of hugs and holds from our family, including her 2-year-old sister and an 11-year-old sister in the beginning.

One of the earliest signs of a sensory-regulation issue

centered around her sleep patterns. I constantly woke up right around 2, 4, and 6 a.m. to nurse her. I knew she wasn't hungry, or at least she shouldn't have been. Yet, she would readily nurse and fall back asleep for just a couple of hours. Her sleep patterns didn't stand out to me, because by then I was a mother of three and felt like I knew what I was doing. Other babies have difficult sleep patterns. Nothing really stood out to me for concern, except that she was never good at taking naps, either. I wondered whether she was really getting enough sleep for her age. She seemed to get by on the bare minimum, which didn't really change throughout her toddlerhood. Now, my oldest was similar in her sleep, so again I wasn't alarmed. Looking back after learning all about sensory diets and sensory regulation, I now question those sleep patterns. Sleep was one area of notice, but then there was also the crashing into anything and everything. She never simply climbed up on the couch. She would run towards it and hug it so tightly, then climb up, roll around, roll off, then repeat. No stepladder was off limits. Her crib was a mini-trampoline, and she was lifting one leg and getting down before 10 months old! I should've realized what was ahead of me, but I didn't at that time.

For her, sensory seeking meant wanting hugs, squeezes, pressure, and tickles in almost every arena, and it was never enough! She developed little games with her siblings and would attempt to tickle them in order to get tickled herself. This insatiable need for the extrasensory support has stayed with her. Some kids are like that and the best thing we can do is to teach them to ask for it when possible and also to self-regulate. Give them as many opportunities for sensory stimulation and regulation as possible.

Bri loved soft furry blankets and still does. When I would see her behaving extremely hyperactive, I heated up the blankets in the dryer for a few minutes, then gave her a big warm hug with the heated blanket. It not only helped her calm down but enabled her to sleep better as well. She often walked around the house when big enough with her own comforter, and hide in it as needed. We had a puppy at the time that she wasn't so sure about, so she covered her whole body up in her comforter, including her head, and peeked out to see what the puppy was doing.

After the crib stage, I always kept stuffed animals, pillows, and extra blankets in her bed so she could cocoon herself as needed. Sometimes, she would hide in her sister's closet under all of those blankets. She still does that if upset, although she takes up a lot more space in the tiny closet. Peek-a-boo and hide and seek became some favorite ways to add language into sensory play. Another area of sensory regulation I noticed in hindsight was her need for her pacifier. All of my girls had pacifiers—some longer than others—so nothing seemed different to me there. The difference with Bri was if she had the pacifier in her mouth, nothing else mattered or registered with her. It was almost too self-soothing.

I came home one day from work, and Bri was wearing a blue- crocheted sweater that her grandmother had knitted. She was happy and content. I took off her little garment and noticed swelling on her wrist the size of a golf ball. I freaked out and took her immediately to the pediatrician. Turns out that she had been stung by a bee or wasp while on a stroller walk with her grandmother, and she hadn't cried one single tear. In fact, she'd shown no discomfort for hours, which wasn't a good sign for sure. She exhibited a delayed or absent pain notification, along with the ability to just keep sucking that pacifier, giving no indication of pain. That lesson taught me to check her whole body from time to time, just to be sure.

Sensory is not only about the soft hugs and squeezes. Sometimes, it's about the pure need to jump up in the air out of nowhere. I believe jumping was one of the most natural ways that Bri developed some more of her language skills. She was entertained by her bigger sister and friends who swung her or jumped up in the air while holding her. They named this game, "Whoopa, Whoopa," because that's what Bri labeled it. Amanda, my oldest, used to play it with her while singing the "Oompa Loompa" song from *Charlie and the Chocolate Factory*, which is how the name of the game was chosen. Good memories— This was her game, the one she named, and it has stuck to this day with our family. As long as Amanda was jumping up and down while holding Bri, it was "whoopa whoopa"–time, and it was great. The social interactions, the language, the relationship building, and all other building blocks were in place for family participation. Fast forward ahead to our current life, and now the roles have been reversed. Bri outgrew her sister by at least four inches and could hold her sister now if she wanted. The wonderful thing is how their relationship with this game and each other has lasted.

The recurring theme for our babies with autism as they are developing is the relationship. Don't ever believe for a minute that there's one child with autism who doesn't want nor need a relationship with their parents, siblings, peer groups, friends, or relatives. That's as furthest from the truth as it can be. Their situations may look different, because they deal with anxiety and have heightened sensory reactions to touch, closeness, light, and sound. These issues are not the same, as only the distance and the timing that we physically approach these issues differs. An actual relationship is built upon during every minute of your child's life. Every glimpse from their peripheral vision, a stem behavior, or even a scream, is our children's way of saying, "Here I am" and "What comes next?".

All behaviors are an attempt at communication and must be translated as that in order to make a true connection. I have professionally seen no less than 50 children with autism in varying environments, and the same is always true. They can run, hide, hit, or perform any number of behaviors, but their body language is their communication, and you need to be listening.

I love meeting a new child with autism and seeing how fast I can find their secret language and ways to communicate. I learned early on in my career before Bri to spend hours watching for the slightest sign of acknowledgment. As a parent, you develop a sixth sense with any of your children, but our kids on the spectrum depend on that even more. As far as slight aggression or hitting, it can be just as much as a surprise to the child as it is to the adult getting hit. With all their behaviors that need to be redirected, aggression needs to be attended to, but not before you try to figure out what the problem is with the child or what they're trying to communicate. With more severe behaviors and aggression, the child must be given reinforcement for appropriate behavior as well as set rules for calm- body behavior.

The teaching of emotions through social stories and other strategies are effective at the pre-teaching moment. When aggression is shown, it must be dealt with in a quick and firm response. While the kids may not mean it, they can't go around biting or hitting, which interferes with their independence faster than anything else. Teach and reinforce the appropriate ways for them express their emotions from the earliest age possible. Be consistent! It's never too early to teach appropriate behavior. Do not allow a young baby even to bite, because it quickly becomes a habit that's hard to break. In some cases, an occupational therapist suggests using oral devices like a chew necklace to help with exaggerated oral needs. When a young child is allowed to bite out of frustration, the possibility of that behavior lasting throughout the older years is not something you'll want to take on.

I often wonder what kind of personal hell it must be for our children on the spectrum. They are trying desperately to get a message to us, yet are not able to, which is why we must work so hard at the basics of communication any way possible. I've seen with the lowest of children that when given the right reinforcement, usually food, you are at least be able to get a hand reach or partial eye contact. Just pay attention to the details, and keep trying. Never give up on a child being able to communicate something to you, because they will eventually. From the slightest gesture, we can build on that next step. The main goal, in the beginning, is to simply achieve basic understanding and some control for the child so they are not constantly frustrated due to unmet needs.

"His ear heard more than what was said to him,

and his slow speech had overtones not of

thought, but of understanding beyond thought."

John Steinbeck

20

Start with the Basics

The most influential speaker I've ever had the privilege of learning from was Dr. Barry Prizant. He changed my life. Bri was about two- or three-years-old when I traveled to Las Vegas to hear him at a conference. I was just coming to terms with the idea of having a child with a disability around this time, so when I listened to him, it was still from the role of a teacher.

Years later, I came to truly appreciate his message in the way I was teaching my own daughter as well as my students. The core of his conference was in presenting his SCERTS model. Basically, Social Communication, Emotional Regulation, Transactional Support or SCERTS is the core for everything we need to help our kids to use their communication and begin to participate in the world around them. In a nutshell, he described how we must look at the basic needs being met first. Is the child hungry, tired, or do they need to go to the bathroom? Is there some tactile sensitivity bothering them? These are questions to consider. Next, he described how to make communication functional by having the child engage in activities that will promote the language. Some of the examples were making popcorn with an air popper. I have used this tool both with Bri and my students throughout the years. It was always a success.

To engage children in an activity, like making popcorn, you'll use the smell and sounds to entice them to the activity. Participating is just fun for them. The language games that come from such an activity are numerous, from teaching the basic P sound to rhyming words. You can also have students make requests for popcorn, label the popcorn, sequence the steps in making it, and more. Use their receptive language, sign language, picture exchange communication system, or any of your current forms of language acquisition with this activity. It's a good strategy to get the most communication and social interaction. Social connection is also key because, as you are making popcorn, you are engaged with your child or a small group. You can do this activity with the child's sibling, but it's geared toward a pairing or group. The excitement that comes from this activity is contagious.

Furthermore, cooking of any kind, making lemonade, gardening, arts, and crafts, are all good options to promote engagement. Anything that requires steps to be taken is excellent. Your goal is to have the children communicate and share in the action with friends. The point is that we have as many opportunities as we create to make the child, who might feel safer by not participating, want to join in on the activity. As long as it appears to be fun, we can entice their little shy spirit to see what's going on in the kitchen or in the classroom. We can make it interesting with scents of food, or by stirring spoon against a bowl or plugging in an appliance to see how a simple machine works. Reinforce the participation, even just a little. Just encourage them to be in the same room if that is where their boundaries lie.

When Bri was younger, she loved to watch me bake

and use a hand mixer. Loved it but was deathly afraid of the noise! I always set the mixer on the lowest speed, and when she hid around the corner, I stopped the mixer. When I saw her peeping around the corner again with curiosity and watching me, I would turn it on again. We had a fun little game going. I'm not so sure about our baked goods, but we always managed to come up with a finished product eventually.

Over time, she began to participate with more responsibility and involvement. I asked her take some steps forward before the noise began to alleviate her anxiety. Next, I gave her the cupcake liners to place in the pan. During that, we labeled colors, counted with one- to-one correspondence, and came up with a finished product.

As a teacher in a school environment, I also implement these important steps with each task that I give to my students as well. The nature of kids on the spectrum is to get the task over as soon as they can, or escape from it whenever possible. Many of my students are still in the dumping stage of development, and when presented with work materials like puzzle pieces, they will promptly throw them under the table or dump them to the side near another student. I try to intervene with this behavior by using mats with their names on them as work boundaries. I also provide them with baskets to hold their puzzle pieces or construction paper tasks, and I make them accountable for keeping their items in their basket. Like all other lessons, this lesson is taught with consistency. With consistency, even the littles learn in routine and develop good work habits.

We definitely have to interfere in their escape, but we also must promote one more minute of involvement and participation, scaffolding these skills until the task is complete. It's very important to teach them that every task has a beginning, a middle, and an end, that we don't stop until we're at the end, if possible. You begin teaching them using baby steps. For example, after getting Bri to place the cupcake liners in the pan, we graduated to her next job. I gave her the ice cream scooper to measure out the batter. She could measure just enough without making a huge mess, and again using the one-to-one correspondence. Each step became her own, and then making cupcakes became her job. Note, this isn't where you should be worried about messes. You can set boundaries, but you want to be very careful about stifling their participation by thinking about the clean-up process. This kind of creative time is important on many levels.

The language opportunities are whatever you make them. With Bri, I asked her to look at the picture prompts on the side of the cake box. She would locate the picture and say, "One, two, three eggs!" I replied, "That's right, three eggs. Now, where are the eggs?" She then would go to the refrigerator, retrieve the eggs, and we would count them together.

Everything is a lesson that can be broken down into as many steps as needed. The first thing taught in special education classes is task analysis. By definition, it means to break down the steps, reinforce as you go, and repeat. Any project or activity that requiring full participation or action can be turned into a social-emotional activity promoting language. Get creative and build on your child's interest inventory.

Numerous craft projects or cooking activities also will lend themselves to this kind of cooperation from your child, and the environment will help you build their language and social connection. I explored the clearance sections in hobby stores just to find something that might spark my daughter's interests. Sometimes, it was a birdhouse to paint or a gingerbread house to assemble, but you get the picture. I'm not a crafty person by nature, although I should be as a teacher. I learned with each child and each project that I didn't need to make it complex. When I first began teaching, Pinterest and stores like Michael's Arts and Crafts or Hobby Lobby didn't exist, as far as I was aware. Teaching and working with children is much more fun and easier with these modern tools and resources. The point is that anyone can do these things. It's not difficult to find an activity to share with your child that will trigger that most desired language and social opportunities.

The "ER" portion of Dr. Prizant's model is the elusive Emotional Regulation. When a child feels safe and their bodies are in control, they are more receptive to learning. Emotional Regulation is another area where you consider first the basic needs of the child. You must make sure there are no underlying issues, such as hunger, sleep, thirst, toileting, allergies, or sickness. Parents are usually tuned in to all of these variables by nature, but teachers also need to consider these basic human needs before starting to teach an activity. (Note, teenagers mimic toddlers as far as sleep and hunger needs, so consider these variables for children of all ages, not just the little ones.)

None of us so-called typical people or adults are beyond the nature of not being exactly emotionally regulated. If you're not feeling well, go to work with a hangover, or just fought with your spouse before work, you will not be the best person at your business that day. The same holds true for our children. In order for them to be the most accessible to what we want to teach them, they must be free of stress or anxiety that can handicap their efforts.

"I've learned that you lean best by modeling. If you want people to learn, do it!!" Leo Buscaglia

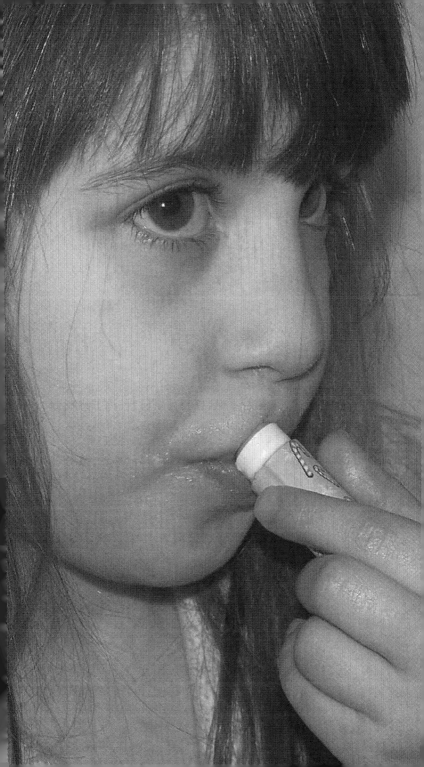

21

Be Your Child's Best Detective

This chapter is directed towards teachers as well as parents who are prepping for their child's learning or the beginning of their school day. Parents sometimes have a clearer picture of the general state of mind or mood their child may be in. These states must be considered, which takes us back to the earlier discussion of knowing your child and doing the necessary detective work at times. Looking for the obvious and not so obvious with our children *before* approaching them with a learning task is not always easy. They don't seem to be communicating any discomfort, but then when presented with a stimulus or request, they fall apart. If we can prevent them falling apart, we are more likely to have success, which translates into success for our kids. When we run into this situation where they're falling apart, we must work backwards to figure out what happened or what the child's perception is, and then work around it.

In my preschool class, for example, sometimes the babies come   in from leaving a parent, or the school bus, completely unraveled.   I mentally go through the list of the usual concerns, checking for hunger, bathroom needs, thirst, and transition issues from parents. Possibly they had too much stimulation from the noisier hallways while coming in or other children irritated them, or they're upset about the social expectation to say hello to people as they come in or another unknown variable. Any number of irritants can occur before the child even enters the classroom.

What if you can't figure it out? Your first line of defense is to calm their little spirit down. You can't negotiate with a very sad or upset three-year-old with logic! You can, though, pick them up, rock them, hold them, and calm them down. When they're ready to face the world, you can then continue with your plans. Even in the home environment, you may not realize as you are rushing around with your morning routine, that your little one wants only pink socks and you've attempted to put on blue socks, and the drama begins. Being aware does not mean you cannot balance your schedule or your own morning routine needs, but at least you can look for the reason that your child has suddenly fallen apart. It would be lovely if we could all be treated a little more genteelly when we're having a rough start to our day.

Why is it so difficult to get our children to participate in the typical tasks that their neurotypical peers do so willingly? Motivation and skill set all play an important role at the beginning of any new tasks, once the earlier obstacles discussed are remedied. For our special children, it's just not a natural setting sometimes to sit down and play with modeling clay or color on paper. Ruling out any sensory issues or obsessions, some of our kids will jump right in with a new task with general interest, but not all of them. How do you figure out your child? If you're a teacher reading this book, how do you figure this out for all of your students?

Previously, I mentioned trying everything. Always remember to keep the task simple at first. If you want to get a child to engage in a coloring activity, for example, then just put one or a few crayons out at a time in basket. In my classroom, I like to use the restaurant baskets that hold a burger and fries, which you can find at most restaurant supply stores. These baskets help organize their space and keeps them from losing their materials. So many of our children either hoard all of the crayons or obsess on peeling the labels off or breaking them. Put aside just a few; it limits the temptation to do all of those behaviors. Then, get a big piece of paper and maybe model a few strokes on the paper to see if they will participate.

With Bri, she was obsessed with *Teletubbies*. So, I would draw the outline in each color of the *Teletubbies*, and yes, we would sing the song. Then she'd continue the drawing on her own. With so many of our children who are more artistically advanced and have a desire to draw, starting a pattern that they want to continue will often get them started with rigor. For our more hesitant artists, it may take some coaxing. I start with giving colors choices between crayons. Or I might ask for help with opening the lid on the modeling clay can to attempt engagement with a shy partner. Once they've started creating, simply try to get short periods of work and don't make the table time too long. Another interesting way to connect with your kids during work time in school, or when you are in a restaurant and your goal is to keep them occupied for a time, is to start a pattern with them. With Bri, and other students of mine, I began by writing A, B, C, and they would have no choice but to complete it due to their insatiable desire to continue the pattern. The same works with numbers or shapes. Whatever was in their repertoire of skills is what I used. This is why drawing the outline of the *Teletubbies* worked with Bri. She had to finish the pattern. If I started with red, she knew that the group had four colors and all of them needed to be represented.

As we look for motivation, reinforcement, and perfecting skills with our kids, it's important to understand that most of our children do not want to complete the task because the teacher or parent suggests it. The motivation belongs to them. An unfinished pattern can be so motivating to complete. These attempts draw their interest to not only multiple activities, but also to sit at the table or any workspace to try new things. It's very important for later independence with school-related activities. Some classrooms are now adopting the idea of flexible seating and moving furniture pieces that are accommodating to our children who need to work with a little wiggle. Still, it's important for attending to the task that our children learn to have a workspace that they need to remain in in order to complete the work goal.

Our children have this window of time, so it's essential to utilize it early on to try to get some baseline skills developing. It's a great time for intervention, especially when we suspect developmental delays, or if we have a diagnosis, while they are young. With autism, we are gaining insight into earlier signs or symptoms, and we need to take advantage of that knowledge and intervene with young children as early on as possible. During this window, they haven't yet had time to develop too many disinterests or reasons not to participate. Everything is fresh in the beginning, and exploring new toys, activities, and materials, and just time at the table is natural and becomes a part of their routine. If you have an older child and you are struggling to get them interested in various activities, you can still try new strategies to motivate them.

I often was surprised by my own child's interests. She never had sensory issues as far as getting wet or sticky and would try to play with clay or paint without concern. I found that she loved tiny things like beads or small marbles that were used to create a picture in some of the craft kits. She must've been only four- or five-years-old and I thought for sure at the time that it would be too advanced for her, but I was wrong! She was really skilled at it and demonstrated a lot of patience filling in all the holes with the marbles until the picture was formed. She also used to do multi-piece jigsaw puzzles on the computer at record speed. I learned this by observing her during an unstructured moment. There are so many activities to help our children to explore with art and table time. Have some fun exploring all the different types of crayons, paint, paper, and clay to see what puts the spark in your little one.

Play is a child's work and such a great way to develop language, fine motor skills, and social development. Not all play must take place at the table. In fact, it shouldn't. Earlier, I mentioned to place art paper on walls or easels to promote working vertically. You can even place under a table so they can create like Michelangelo, by drawing at an upward angle while lying on their backs. Play or exploration with art can take place anywhere and it should. Floor time is the best time, especially with our younger children, to spend lots of time exploring toys, looking at books, and practicing their play skills. It's also an important time for siblings and parents in which to participate. Although many of our children are quite content playing with one or two items by themselves, you should interfere from time to time. Even while playing, if a child seems hyper-focused on a toy, say   for example a rattle, you can take the opportunity to label it and   its color and sound, giving yourself a turn, and then your child. In every moment, a learning task can take place simply by adding a language, a little interest, and participation. This modeling behavior shows our children what the toy is and how we play with it, which is a much more natural experience with typically developing children. Most parents wouldn't find it necessary to put that much thought into their child's play. However, with our children needing a lot more language support and social skill development, it needs to   be broken down into smaller steps that will help our kids build a hierarchy toward appropriate play skills and language acquisition.

"The capacity to learn is a gift; the ability to learn is a skill; the willingness to learn is a choice." Brian Herbert

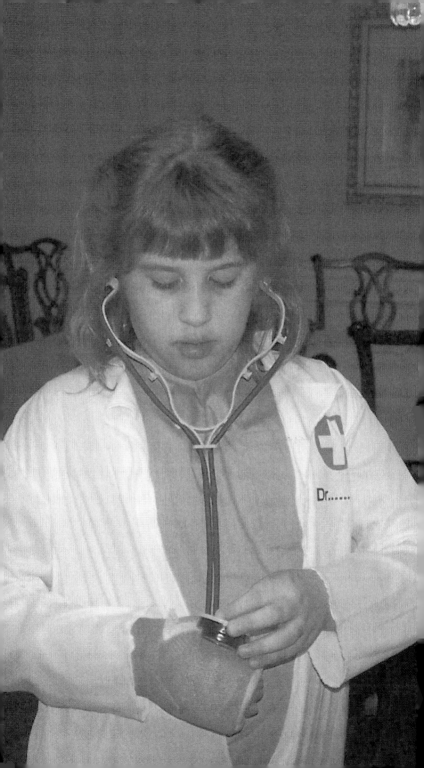

22

Getting Down to Business

Where do you begin? You may have just been given a diagnosis from your pediatrician. You may have been watching the signs like I did for the longest time and wondered, and then ignored them. Once you have that first inkling of anything wrong with any of your children, your mind begins to try to make sense of it all and fix it as quickly as you can.

Let's talk about the steps that come before that. As you notice delays in your child with attention or listening, you'll first work with your pediatrician to rule out the basic medical possibilities. Vision, hearing, and even further investigation into other medical concerns can help determine what is a medical problem and what is a developmental delay. With Bri, I saw her selective hearing in action when she was around age one. Other family members told me that she was acting like she couldn't hear, but I knew that wasn't the case. If Elmo was on the television upstairs and she was downstairs, Bri would follow the sound until she found Elmo's voice or picture.

Her hearing was not the issue. Still, hearing is usually the first thing to screen. Usually, a general pediatrician cannot assess hearing at this age. I recommend seeing an ear, nose, and throat (ENT) specialist, or going to a pediatric speech and language clinic where they use all the bells and whistles to really evaluate hearing. The same goes for other medical conditions that may co-exist with autistic-like behaviors. Once you've determined what you are up against, it's time to begin the work. Attention is key in all therapy. During this time, you're going to become the constant in your child's life and focus. They're already your world and you are theirs, which will be shown through the visible interaction that you control on a daily basis. I don't know if I did consistently with Bri. If I knew then what I know now and would, if given a second chance at her early years. I am attentive daily now with the other young children in my classroom, starting from the very first open house at the beginning of the school year. I enter their world, whether I am invited or not! I invade their space in the most fun way possible. If it's not possible, I invade their world anyway. As their parents, you need to be best buddies with them, and that's what you're going to create with your child. Every time you see them, every nap they wake up from, and every tantrum they participate in, you will be the constant. This is not much different from typical parenting, except that you don't get much of a break! Don't forget to ask your team or your village for them, because obviously you will need breaks. Attention looks different with each child, but with children with autism, eye contact is not always easy to get as mentioned before. Sometimes you must settle for approximations of attention. If it looks like they are listening or watching you from their peripheral vision, then accept it. You need to know that they'll respond to your voice, touch, and smell when you request it. Basically, you can't teach language or anything else if you don't have their attention. Attention is top priority. Our babies are experts at avoidance and escape even from a young age. Trust me, I have witnessed the Houdini's and very skilled escape artists at any age to avoid the work that is required of them. These children are highly intelligent and skilled at manipulation, so you must be aware of the foundation you are trying to put into place. You have to work to get them to participate in your demands of attention.

Every child and every parent will have their own special way of interacting, depending on their personalities and interests. I am very dramatic in my therapy style, and some kids eat it up. Some find it overwhelming, so I tune it down at times. I am consistent. If I call the name of a child and get no response, I will try anotherway to get them to respond. Sometimes a prop can be used to seek their attention. Food can also be used—anything that you pair is utilized with the goal of getting the child's attention. I share this not only because of the importance, but also because it's not always as easy as it sounds. When I held a bottle or the pacifier or when nursing Bri, I also spoke her name. When I carried on a soothing conversation or sang to her, I paired it with a reinforcement, my request for her attention. I received it from her beautifully, every time. I remember it, but I also realize that I wasn't looking for her reply to be any different from my previous two children. I had no idea that autism was in the wings. Later in her life, it was not as easy to gain her attention. She was very skilled and selective when and at what she would listen to, including her mother!

I often used a small musical instrument like a maraca or a bell to catch her attention, because she loved music and anything to do with it. I sang her songs or pretended to read her favorite books, then I would wait to see if she would sit next to me. I would eat something meant for her and say, "mmm," until she looked up to see what I was eating. I also played peek-a-boo with a scarf or blanket, and tried to get her to participate. The main idea is that you are the most interesting person or playmate in your child's life! You want them to always want to stay near to you so they don't miss out on a party! Once you have this captive audience, you can begin to help develop those language and social skills.

So once the attention of your child is established, what is your next step? For most of us, early intervention happens naturally because we don't yet know there's a need for it. Before an official diagnosis, most parents are singing, talking, playing and reading to their kids. It's also the same once told our child has a delay. We simply have to amp it up by about a thousand volts slowly over time. Our children can be easily overwhelmed or overstimulated, so you don't want to address a toddler with hours of direct therapy. If you do, you'll have an emotional mess on your hands. You must pace yourself, and your child will follow your lead. Involve their interests in what you are showing them. Use caution and be aware of how long they want to participate. More is not always better in these sessions. Consistency is more important. You can talk about a ball for two minutes, but do it several times a day every day until the child understands. Each child has his or her own pace, as well as tolerance for group time, even if the group is just you and them. Observe these variables and be sensitive to them, as they will expand over time.

"Mama was my greatest teacher, a teacher of compassion, love and fearlessness. If love is sweet as a flower, then my mother is that sweet flower of love." Stevie Wonder

23

Communication in the Natural Environment

You will want to label everything in the natural environment several times a day. It's not that your child needs items labeled. You do   it because you're teaching them the sound and the meaning of language and how to use it.

Every time I switched on a light with Bri as a toddler, I let her touch the switch or flip it on and off. I labeled the light, and said, "Turn on the light, turn off the light." It sounds redundant at times, but it's how they recognize the label and begin to make it their own vocabulary.

The more vocabulary they own at a young age, the better their communication skills develop. Not only should you be labeling items around the house, but also the functions of things and the relationships in your household. Label people in your house, including the family pet. Name the grandparents who may live out of state. Simply label everything. In addition to labeling everything, show them pictures for all of the language, too. Visual prompts are secret treasures for all of our children. The pairing of a picture of anything that you're labeling, or the object itself, solidifies the label in the brains of our children with communication delays. It makes it easier for them to process, remember, and use the vocabulary. I've spent numerous hours making pictures, laminating them, and using Velcro on them to create visual prompts for my daughter and for my students. The creation of visual prompts is the basis for all of our essential prep work with language. Over the course of my parenting and career, those visuals have changed drastically with Google images, cellphone cameras, and tablets, but the basis is the same. We're lucky to live in such an era now with technology, because the whole world is using visual imagery for everything. It isn't therapy but our natural environment as we know it.

Within some of our basic assessments for language ability, we, as educators, ask students to label 10, 50, or a 100 and more basic words, consisting of food, animals, colors, household items, and other basics. It is why parents must start labeling in the natural environment. Even reading is a visual memory process. Although some kids learn phonetically as well as sight read, our children on the spectrum usually are primarily sight-word readers. Bri often surprised me what she could "read" based on her preferences. During a Google search on her tablet at a very early age, she could put enough letters together to spell out, *Bear in the Big Blue House* using predictive typing. Even recently while browsing my car radio for the choices of her favorite songs, she located and found what she seeking. In isolation, I'm not sure these skills would be as strong for her, but when it comes to what she wants, she can configure it out with just the printed word and no pictures. I believe it's because she stills sees the paired visual in her mind and memory. Pictures and words are the same for her—it's all visual memory strength—a type of visual memory like a picture taken that's stored.

I remember being quite frustrated with teaching her to read or at least attempting. I bought every set of books, the basic skills readers, the leveled readers, and books with high interest and low vocabulary. I used all the strategies that teachers use, and I was failing with my daughter teaching her that way. I had scheduled times to read with her during the day, and before bedtime, I had extensive library visits with special baskets for library books. I kept separate containers for home books, and I was always rewarding all my girls with a trip to the bookstore. These were actually the same habits I had in place with my other girls, which gave them a fantastic love of reading. However, it didn't work with Bri! She would speed read, flipping pages at record speeds to be able to announce to me, "The end!"

The dilemma is that sometimes the way our children absorb information is so different from typical children, but they do get it. Research shows that repetition is important for remembering stories and increasing vocabulary and comprehension. Don't be discouraged with their flipping of pages or the throwing of books. Start simply and make it routine. Just as you would with teeth brushing and bath time, read on a regular schedule daily. Read the same stories, especially the classics. Read stories like *The Three Little Pigs*, *Goldilocks and the Three Bears*, and *Red Riding Hood* to build on the rhythm of stories. Have your child label the characters. You can also have them predict what comes next. If possible, label the beginning, middle, and ending of each story. Use pictures to sequence the stages found in the stories. Label everything that they see in the pictures of the books. Literacy is different for our children on the spectrum, but it is not an impossible feat. Most of our children are very interested in learning their letters, and often are self-taught by learning sight words. For our children, it may or may not look like sitting down and enjoying a book. As in every other area, consistency is key. If at first, they don't show any interest in reading, try an audio of the story in the background to enable them become familiar with the sound of the story's language. Usually, it's the visual delight from the books that holds their interests.

I am old-fashioned when it comes to a good book. I like to hold and read it. Nowadays, we have stories on tablets for read-aloud books, which are great and should be used. Use all forms of reading to help children build their inventory of stories. Reading is the stepping stone for all things academic. Remember, at first children read for developing interests and skills. But later in school, they read for information in science and social studies. Bri, still to this day, will try to tell me things in her echolalia language through stories. If her food is hot, she might bring up the *Three Little Bears*. She'll repeat the part about the Mama bear saying, "It's too cold," and you'll see the pattern. I also think she enjoyed the stories like all children do.

To summarize the beginning of home therapy (or what I like to call my life), everything you introduce our children to, whether it's the basic repeating of sounds or words, the labeling of common objects, or reading, it must be done systematically. You likely will never go into a hobby store and look at materials like pom-

poms or craft sticks the same way again. You'll learn that everything can be made into a better visual prompt to gain their attention.

"A picture is worth a thousand words" is an accurate saying, but for our population a picture is a key to understanding. Visual strategies are essential to helping children with autism understand faster and more comprehensively. As a teacher, when I am teaching reading using the story *The Three Little Bears*, the week's activities would appear as follows. We would read the story with as much drama and passion as possible. Next, I would point out the characters through the pictures. Then, I would read the story traditionally. I would show a read -aloud, and then find a matching bear song from the internet. At the math table, I would have the children sort bears into size and colors. They would take the same bears and act out the story with the help of a blonde barbie doll to replicate Goldilocks. We could also cook porridge. I would have the students use wooden blocks and pictures of the three differently sized bears to measure the bears and label them big, medium, or small. Basically, you must use all learning modalities to help children understand the language concepts and communication.

"We are all apprentices in a craft where no one ever becomes a master." Ernest Hemingway

24

Social Stories

Let's take a deeper look at visual strategies that are used to introduce social stories. Carol Grey started Social Stories, an excellent social learning tool for children and adults with autism and other communication disorders. Her work began a foundation for the use of social stories to enhance understanding, reduce conflict, and to help children with autism navigate through many different environments. A social story is a tool where you give a visual example of what is to be expected. For example, a trip to the hair salon dentist or doctor might be anticipated with less anxiety by providing a child with a social story.

I take pictures of everything, so does my mother. Everyone in the family complains about this until the day comes where they sit down and look at the cherished family albums. They relive special vacations or memories that could have been forgotten without these photos. Bri even enjoys looking at the family albums and seeing the trips to see Mickey Mouse or the beach. She even uses them to request and tell us that she's ready for a vacation. Unfortunately, it doesn't work like that with many of our schedules. The point of my story is that a picture is a representation of so many emotions, and it's wonderful to have them. In a social story, the pictures become more about pairing a lesson with a story. A social story explains the sequence of events, and the before and after of a visit. They serve as a compass to navigate what is to be expected of a child who cannot simply be told that they are making a visit to someplace. I used to struggle with taking Bri to get her thick, curly hair cut. I would take her to the kid's salon, and allow her to indulge in multiple lollipops much to my regret. Yet, it would do little to reduce her anxiety as a stranger was coming at her with sharp scissors!

On one trip to the salon, I took pictures, lots and lots of pictures. I took happy ones, sad ones, mad ones, and even chaotic ones. I took pictures of the lollipops, the bathroom, the books in the waiting area, and the nice lady who was going to cut her hair. These pictures were taken with a camera. I probably looked like a lunatic to the other families in the waiting room, but I did it anyway. The pictures were developed and printed. I put them together in a photo album. I tried to put them in some order, and then printed scripts to describe the visit.

Over time, I made these photo albums a little more sophisticated. The mission was to make a book to help Bri understand the whole process the next time she needed a haircut. She enjoyed labeling herself, of course, as well as the lollipops and the little horse chair that children sit in. I then described in simple vocabulary that she doesn't need to cry. I told her that she had such pretty hair, and that big girls get haircuts. The words you use in the explanation must be appropriate for your child. If your child's behavior is the main concern with a haircut, talk about it. If their anxiety is high, use calming and relaxing vocabulary. The strength in your own personal social stories is the investment that your child makes in their story. The predictability of the next visit, the expected behavior, and what the task at hand is are the concepts to be covered. If necessary, a reinforcing element can be built into the story, as long as you can be consistent every time. It's possible that every haircut warrants an ice cream cone. It's up to you, but don't put anything into writing or pictures that you won't be able to stand behind. Some of the photo websites will spiral bound together your stories. They make cute little portable books that you can keep with you and review with your child when necessary. The main focus for your family is to keep a visual representation personalized for your child, your event, and your child's needs. You then make that story your own. The outcome will be helpful in more circumstances than you can ever imagine.

I made books for Bri, and many of my students through the years, for medical appointments, planned and unplanned. Hair appointments; birthday parties; family events; and visits to the library, a puppet show, and a circus are all events where social stories can be used. You will use this tool for your sanity and for the benefit of your child. Using social stories is always helpful. It isn't difficult to write or create your own social stories that fit your needs. Helpful online resources of ready-made social stories also exist, and they can be used with your child or in your classroom to assist with general behaviors and some other issues. However, for your purposes, I want the social stories to be personalized with your child as the star in their own life story. Bri's social stories from her early years are now used as language review and an opportunity to talk about memories. She has a storybook about when we first brought home our puppy. In this book, the fear in Bri's face over this bouncy blonde bundle in our living room, and her escaping to cover her entire body in a big blanket, created wonderful memories now, but they now serve a different purpose. We lost our sweet beautiful Golden Retriever Josie, so I am blessed now to have that book of Josie's puppyhood, even though it was created for therapeutic reasons at that time. There are so many times after the social stories served their purpose that both my daughter and my many students loved their personalized social stories because these stories were about them. Both my daughter and students like to go through the memorized pages over and over again, each enjoying their story for a different purpose. One particular student always wanted to take off all of her clothes on the playground at recess. I created a book for her which included all the most adorable princess dresses that a five-year-old little girl would enjoy. That social story helped her understand that pretty outfits on at school. She can change her clothes at home. She can take them off only to have a fun bubble bath, and then to put her pajamas on. Clothes stay on for most of the day. After reading the social story with her daily right before scheduled outdoor playtime, she finally understood the behavioral expectations for recess and school. She would repeat her story back to anyone who would listen. The lesson was learned.

I put together another social story for a three-year-old who was insistent upon immediately taking her shoes off once in the classroom. This beautiful little girl would walk in, and the very next moment she was barefooted. While it wasn't as awkward as taking off all the clothes on the playground, but it still wasn't appropriate for school. For her, I made a social story about all kinds of shoes. I made visuals for boots, slippers, rain boots, Mickey and Minnie shoes, flower shoes, and rainbow shoes. She loved looking through her own personal fashion magazine and pointed to her feet with every picture. She got the message—shoes stay on! We accomplished that obstacle without taking any power away from this little princess. Simple strategies can be personalized for each situation. One of my favorite strategies for potty training is with a social story that we actually use while potty training. I made a story for a very intelligent, but very stubborn little boy whose mother was expecting. He was very capable but not willing to participate fully in the potty-training process. His social story let him know how much of a big boy he was. I put photos of big boys wearing Spiderman underwear and babies wearing diapers. I took pictures of this five-year-old participating in all of his amazing school activities. I took pictures of him reading books, writing on paper, and hanging from the bars on the playground. I included a picture of every event in his big kid world. I also included pictures of bathroom signs, toilets, sinks, and stars for reinforcement on his potty chart. This story was his, and he told everyone about the great things he could do all by himself. Success can be achieved through social stories time and time again. Visual strategies or supports are not limited to photos in books. Endless opportunities can be used to support your child's language building and understanding of his or her universe. Craft sticks with letters to spell out a child's name or pictures from a story to retell a story are all examples of visual strategies to aid with instruction.

An eloquent frame of reference for visual supports is Temple Grandin's book titled, *Thinking in Pictures*. This book revolutionized how our children see, hear, and repeat back what they are exposed to. Their minds work like cameras, taking in the information and giving it back at the right opportunity. Ten to twenty years ago, this concept wasn't as apparent as it is now. Everything in our world is visual. This is the norm for everyone, not just our special population of children. Our visual world can be overwhelming, with all of the stimuli bombarding us at all times. Be strategic in how you utilize visual supports for your child. Remember that in most cases, less is more for understanding with small children, and you can build on the foundation as the child develops.

"How wonderful it is that nobody need wait a single moment before starting to improve the world." Anne Frank

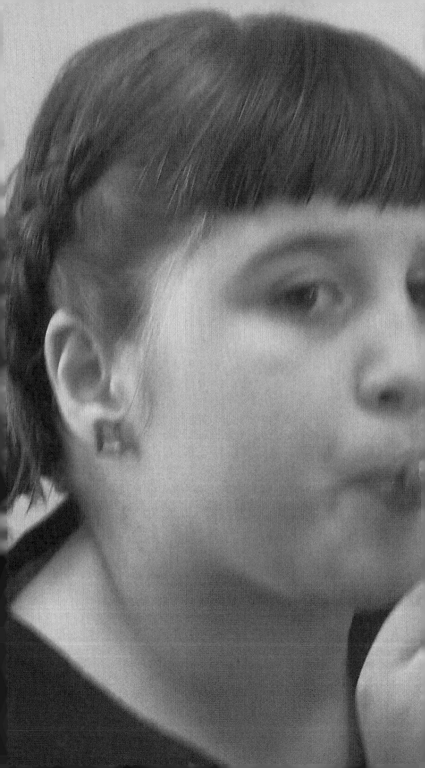

25

Purposeful Listening

*Our children with communication delays of any kind
are speaking to us. We must attend to that
communication.*

I know I didn't ask to be a mother of a baby with
special needs. I did, however, want to be a special
education teacher my entire life—it's my journey. I've
seen the hidden messages from hundreds of children
in my career, and of course, with my own daughter.
Magic happens when I meet a new student with autism
at this point in my career. I see a child with a hidden
personality inside that I look forward to meeting.
Sometimes, I feel like an autism whisperer, and other
times I am faced with the reality that I have a lot of
work ahead of me with that child. I used to welcome
the challenge in my early career, but after personally
struggling with all of the anxiety of raising a child on
the spectrum, I know better. Yes, it's a challenge; it's

more work that has to be done in preparation for this child's ability to thrive and make the connections necessary access his or her world.

Teachers, therapists, parents especially, and more people from your designated village have work ahead of them. The child also has hard work ahead. It will be difficult and complex, but this work is worth every therapy session, every task, and even every struggle. Sometimes you'll work on something with a child for the longest time, and just when you think you need to change course, you'll see a light. It might be a behavioral change, some new attention to the task, or even just a glimmer of understanding. It will take you back to the magic.

The magic always will appear; it comes in various ways. When you least expect it, a door will open or maybe a window will crack, but it's a start. Learning will take place, and connections will be made. No exact formula works for every child, but I believe some key factors do influence the growth of the child. It's difficult for me to separate what I know from my master's degree in special education, 30 years of teaching experience, and the most importantly, being Bri's mom. I know babies need to be held closely. They need soft touches, baby lotion, and gentle massages to their little feet. Most of our children who exhibit severe sensory or tactile defensiveness don't demonstrate these needs at this early stage of life.

I know you should play all kinds of music for your child. I know you should sing to your baby while in utero. I know you should rock your babies to sleep each and every night to lullabies. If you're lucky enough to have a multilingual family, you can sing your baby in all of your mother tongues. I know that when your child's six months of age, you should read rhythmic stories to your child. I know that nutrition is essential during and after pregnancy. I know that rest is essential for your child and you, as well. I know that a peaceful environment is healthy for every member of the family.

Life is complex. I believe in family and support for the whole family, including the primary caretakers, and I believe you need to actively seek out respite from time to time. If you're married, I think you need to have a date night and separate vacations from children. I believe you should have hobbies and interests of your own as a person that you can occasionally pursue. I believe that once you know your path is going to be different from the one planned, you should seek out the best medical therapeutic team that you can. Secondly, you should join a support group for your child's age group. Continue going as your child grows, and stay connected to the ones who share your journey. Honestly, I am telling you this from experience. Half of what I tell you, I didn't do! You should do it, though because it helps. The difference in how I raised a young baby into toddlerhood and beyond didn't differ from my other two girls until I knew it had to. Once therapy was the central line of defense, things changed. I then learned that the work was never ending. The work meant there would be no event in my life that didn't have the word *autism* in it.

It was a new world that I thought I knew until I sat at

the opposite side of the Individual Education Plan (IEP) meeting. I was enlightened, learning that every time I took my baby for a walk in her stroller, I had to label everything on our path. I told her, "Look at the tree. Is that a red bird?" or "What sounds does the birdie make?". Everything became a language lesson in high definition. Nothing was random in the raising of this precious soul.

Time was not my friend. At the time, I didn't even realize how much work was ahead of me. The work, as referred to earlier as play, is found in every activity, every story, and every song. Work is anything that involves teaching your child something new. Work takes place at every meal and when every new guest visits your home. Work is the reduction of anxiety when you use a vacuum cleaner or blender. Work is everything you do with your child to help them navigate in their environment.

Buckle down, because this work is never ending and exhausting! This is why you need to create your team or your village. I cannot overstate the need for your support. It's also why you will look at everything you do with your child as an instructional opportunity. That being said, you still have to enjoy your life, and you will. This book isn't about scare tactics or how difficult it is to train your child with special needs. I have enjoyed every second of raising my daughter, except for some occasional mishaps that usually involve plumbing. To be honest, I have enjoyed and had a blast teaching   so many different students with various levels of autism They are beautiful and intelligent children. They teach us, and we teach them a little, but they hold the secrets of the universe. I say this because, in their innocence, we learn about what is really important in this world. You will have a child. A child with autism, maybe, but also a child who will delight you like any other child, sometimes more! It's in the work where you'll have to think outside of the box with most of your experiences.

You'll go to a playground and consider the safety of your child first, by looking around to see if it is fenced in to give your baby some freedom. You will look at playground equipment as a strategy to help with your sensory needs or the development of gross motor skills, and not view it as just a day at the park. You may go to a puppet show or a movie with your young toddler and cringe at the idea of them screaming out at the top of their voices at the quietest moment. You will worry about what others think of a child who is screaming or out of control. You may stop going to restaurants for a while, but this will pass. You and your child have every right to be wherever you want to be— it where work will feel like war at first. Eventually, you and your child will develop skills and a rhythm to your life. You will be in the world participating like everyone else. You will try new things and find out what works best for you and your family. Again, ask for the help. It doesn't mean you aren't strong enough. It means the process is difficult.

I can't imagine how I would have handled the early years and exploring taking her places if I had not been in a teaching position that taught community-based instruction for most of my career. In other words, my job was to take students with autism everywhere in the community. I taught them to behave, communicate, and socialize in every setting, or at least I tried. With my colleagues, I went with them to grocery stores, puppet shows, movies, restaurants, hiking, zoos, and aquariums. I have no doubt that all the many experiences I had taught me skills and gave me the grace that I would never have developed on my own. Be kind to yourself. It's a journey. It is your learning experience as much as your child's.

I remember many parents telling me while my children were still little, that they could not go to a grocery store with their child. The horror stories they revealed of my students going into stores and taking things or having severe tantrums were crippling to these families. The sad thing was that I was taking these same children into the same places and more, and hardly ever seeing a glimpse of those reactions. Could there be such a diverse interpretation of the same child between home and school? Of course, there was. The reason they differed is due to the prep work.

We prepared these same kids for a week with visual strategies, behavioral modeling, and the excitement of a reward from the bakery before we ventured out. A therapist and teachers then accompanied us to provide support both physically and instructionally. It's obvious that there are two sides to these situations. The parent had limited time to complete the chore of doing the family grocery shopping, possibly with a car full of kids. The parent may have worked all day or had a long shopping list. The parent had only herself for support. The point is, for this example, that the preparatory work needed to be inserted. The child needed to be taught. So much prep work must go into taking your child places.

In the beginning, venturing can be an explosion of stimuli that he or she just can't handle. You start there. If the screams, tears, or meltdowns reoccur in a certain store, play detective and figure it out. Maybe your child fears the baby seat in the cart? Many of our babies have gravitational fears. In other words, sensory deficits make them feel panicky about being placed up high in the cart. Bri had such a fear. She was okay in the shopping cart if I had placed her in one of those comfortable quilted covers that you put in the cart's seat. Without it, she panicked and didn't feel safe. She also never let me change her on a standard changing table. So much of this I learned in hindsight. It may not be easy to figure out why a child tolerates one store over another. It could be the fluorescent lighting, noisy carts, loud people, or anything else that could be overstimulating. Such problematic things can send our children into a frenzy that seems to come out of nowhere. This reaction could happen sometimes, but not all the time. Again, you'll have to play sleuth in these situations. Sometimes, you will go shopping because you need to and just deal with the possible outcomes. I had another parent who told me that their son would continually stare at the grocery store's linoleum flooring. They were correct, he did that. On a few of our outings, he sat on the floor looking at it. I had five other students with me, and I didn't have time for his perseveration. I told him to get off of the floor, and then I put both of his hands on the cart's handle.

He was middle-school aged and tall enough to push the cart. My next strategy was to race through the aisles with him at racing speed. There was no time to gaze at the flooring. He had fun, too, and his mood changed to joy, and it was distracting enough to change directions on his behavior.

Make visits functional! With my own daughter being the youngest of three, and all of them being so young, I also shopped with practicality. I almost never had time to worry about the behavior of any of my children while at the store. I had shopping to do so we could have dinner! All parents struggle with young children in these situations, but this is why we must put the time in that prep work when they are little. For all of my girls, shopping was an event—a learning opportunity to explore all the colors of fruits and vegetables, remembering the milk, and picking out a treat.

For the first two years of Bri's life, I was still thinking and praying that she only had a bit of a speech delay. Once my life became about full-blown autism, I became much more detailed and diligent about even with a trip to the grocery store. To this day, I still have Bri weigh the apples and count out how many oranges to put into a bag. I have her follow a list if we have it, or we just name the items that we need to pick up and make it into a scavenger hunt to find those things. She also helps me put food into the cart. She loads the food into bags and puts it away when we get home. I can assure you this occurs due to the work we did when she was three! Every task builds on the next. Every skill builds on the foundation of their future independence. The work can be tedious, but eventually it pays off. Do the work!

"I may not have gone where I intended to go, but I think I have ended up where I needed to be."

Douglas Adams

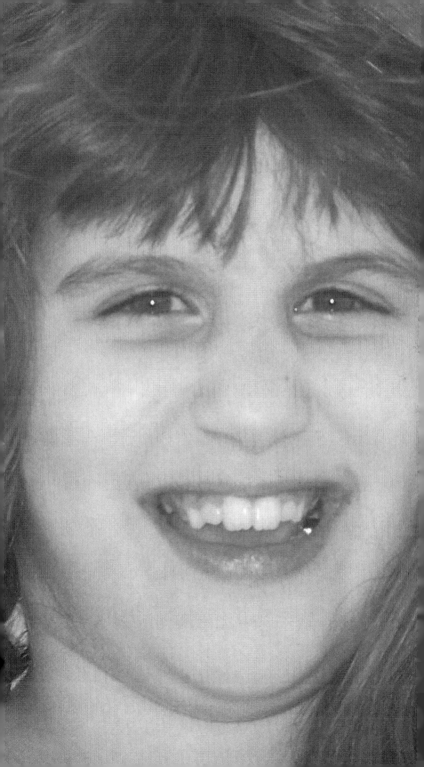

26

Mind-Reading Parenting

One of the most difficult things for parents with children on the autism spectrum can be how to tell when your child is hurt or sick, especially when it isn't obvious.

Due to various sensory deficits, our kids can have an over- or under-arousal to pain or illness. They could have a sore throat for days, but not feel it or not show symptoms. They can get cut and not even realize that they are bleeding or have a delayed reaction to pain.

Bri rarely demonstrated any kind of discomfort if she got hurt, until she saw a bandage, then she would cry. The sight of the bandage was the signal for pain. Once, she stepped on a glass frame that had fallen from the wall. The frame cracked, and she got a sliver of glass in the bottom of her foot. The following moments after this incident, she kept saying, "Tickle, tickle" repeatedly. She still uses that term today when she's in pain or uncomfortable. At that time, she wasn't using that word to describe anything except the real meaning of tickle during play. So, when I went into her room and saw glass all over the floor, I panicked! I lifted her up on to the bed and desperately tried to find out where she was cut. I am sure this has happened to you already. It's always important for you to continually help your child identify illness or pain whenever possible.

In addition, I have used other strategies as well to identify pain. One is a genius idea from one of my dear friends and former assistant. She designed a color-coded large paper doll to replicate the parts of the body. I used this paper doll idea with my daughter and had her label the parts of her body. I then used it preventively to label her tummy, throat, arms, legs, and head. I wanted to teach her to give me information and locations of pain or illness.

Currently, we have apps that can do this as well, but the important thing is be able to teach the children the parts of their body and have them at least receptively identify them when necessary. My other children spiked fevers with most illnesses, especially with strep throat or an ear infection, but not Bri. She was always a veryplayful and happy, so unless an affliction was really obvious, she keeps on acting like herself. Her energy level was always high and steady, so even an illness didn't reveal itself with a behavior change. Without a fever, it was hard for me to know that she was even a little bit ill. What saved me in these circumstances, I believe, was that my two youngest were only two years apart and usually in the same school. If my middle child became ill, then I would also take Bri to the pediatrician as well to have her checked out. As far as reducing anxiety about medical issues, you can use social stories that you personalize for your child, or use readily available books or *Sesame Street* episodes with titles like "Elmo visits the Doctor" or "Elmo visits the Dentist", along with many other supports on the internet. These strategies help with conveying information about what to expect at these visits, as well as reduce anxiety. Some children can get so worked up about going to the medical office that they avoid letting you know they are ill or purposely not tell you due to anxiety of where being sick may lead them to.

I had one student who thought, due to a previous ambulance trip, that ambulances would rush to get him due to any kind of illness or injury. He would panic, and it was very difficult to convince him that this was not the case every time. With Bri, each time we rode on the highway in the direction of the dentist office, she panicked. I then had to tell her where we going and provide pictures that we were on the highway, but it was not the day for the dentist. These social stories helped with a lot of drives, because if I took her to a show or something special, and the trip was on the highway, the next time we were in the car she thought we were repeating that trip as well. Children with autism really need support with visuals or social stories to help them predict their day. Most of us want to know what is expected when we get in the car and where we might be going as a passenger, with these children it's the same, only with increased anxiety.

In both cases, this reaction stems from overgeneralization, which so common with our kids. They believe that if something happens one day, it will happen the same way each time. It's typical for all children and some adults to think that a bad event can occur or reoccur at other times. The problem is that our children on the spectrum are much more difficult to reason with and to explain that the outcome will be different from other times. They are all about patterns, and patterns repeat. Life may repeat in their minds in the same order.

It is good practice to check your child over from head to toe at bath or bedtime. I can't tell you how many times I didn't notice a rash starting or a bruise on Bri's leg right away. When she was wearing long sleeves and jackets in the winter and started to develop a certain kind of eczema, I missed it at first. I changed her right into pajamas, and with more coverage of her body, I didn't see anything of concerned. In the light of the morning, I saw redness all over her extremities. I didn't know if it worsened during the night, and I didn't know how I missed it in the beginning. Another time, Bri kicked her legs up and down underneath her desk at school and began coming home with big bruises on both of her legs in the same area. I visited the school, trying to figure out what was happening. I watched how she was plowing her little legs into the bar and demonstrating absolutely no awareness on this harsh impact. It didn't even faze her.

You won't catch everything, but keep an eye out for undiscovered bruises, marks, or even insect bites as much as you can. This is not only advice for when they are young but for most of their lives. It's difficult, but it's better than our children getting hurt or sick and it getting worse. It definitely beats the mother's guilt I developed when I missed those signs. As mother, we have enough of that guilt without needing any extra.

Another cautionary principle is to always use your best judgement and err on the side of too much, rather than less. In other words, if a child falls and gets hurt, unless you saw him fall on feathers or a mattress and can't possibly be injured, then get them checked out by your pediatrician as soon as possible. Due to the way our kids feel pain and the way they interpret pressure, they could break a bone, and you wouldn't ever know it with their lack of response. I am not suggesting that you have to run to the hospital with every injury, but if the signs are there with redness or swelling, then follow through.

One night when Bri was around six, she ran into my room from the hallway to come to me. She was always running at top speed, and in a somewhat tornado form with her hands flailing, and she always hit the stairwell posts with a touch. That particular night I heard a loud noise as she ran to me. She had really smacked the post with the back of her little hand! She didn't cry! She just looked star struck. I checked her out from head to toe. Her hand started to swell but just a little. I put ice and kept ice on it. The next morning, she said, "Tickle, tickle hand" repeatedly, so off we went to the doctor. She had cracked a bone in her finger. Next, came the nightmare of a lifetime. After the X-rays were taken at the nearest facility, we were told she needed a cast. Nothing is simple with our kids.

I had chosen a big franchise that specialized in orthopedics. I wish; however, I had driven the extra 15 miles to the Children's Healthcare of Atlanta, but I was trying desperately to get her fixed and back to school and myself back to work. I didn't think she had broken anything. I only went to rule it out. Yes, she'd broken a bone in her hand, and yes, a cast was needed.

On my way to this facility, I called the front desk and explained that my daughter had autism. I continued to state that she could be frightened, and therefore, I would need everything explained to me before it was done so that I could prepare her. Once there, I repeated my concerns to the receptionist who I signed her in with, as I filled out the paperwork. A male nurse came and got us for the X-rays. I explained it all to him, again, in detail. I explained my daughter's fears, her interests, and her love of Elmo. I asked for a teddy bear with the broken arm and the color wheel so she could choose her favorite color for the cast. She chose pink. I explained everything to the best of my ability to protect my child and to make it as least stressful as possible. Yet, what happened was while putting the cast on Bri, he brought out the loudest tool possible with no warning and no communication to me, and it completely freaked her out!

First offense—I had told him to tell me each and every step before commencing, and he completely disregarded that request and kept moving with this noisy object towards my baby with autism! I was not a happy mother, to say the least. We survived this stupidity, though, and went home with a little pink cast on my precious but shaken up little angel.

Later that night, Bri began freaking out about something under the cast, and she clawed at it like a little-injured creature. I didn't know what the problem was, but I knew that her saying tickle did not mean tickle, and that something was wrong. I took her back to the facility the next morning as soon as they opened, demanding that they check her out and ensure she wasn't allergic to the materials or simply figure out what was wrong. Again, came the same nurse with a loud and spinning saw, this time to remove the cast and check her out. Well, of course, Bri lost her mind over the noise and began jumping all over the place.

The nurse told me that he'd done this a million times, and yet he again completely ignored my requests. In addition, he was negligent and didn't use the tool that is placed under the cast before he cut. Bri also was not able to sit still like he ignorantly instructed. He began quickly sawing away at the cast, and in the meantime ever so slightly, he cut a fine line into her precious tiny hand.

I was looking at this scene in complete shock, just questioning myself as to what would happen if I just jumped this nutcase right in the doctor's office. He realized his mistake and was apologetic, and continued with the proper safety protocol, but it was too late. Bri had been cut and was traumatized. She still has a scar from it.   I was beside myself in trying to interpret what had just happened and what went wrong. The doctor entered, trying to make amends in quite a nervous fashion, but he spoke to my deaf ears. We left the office! I followed through with the aftercare and went home and cried for both of us.

After the cast was officially removed and her hand had healed, the same doctor called me to offer plastic surgery at his personal expense. I probably had a liability case of some kind, but truthfully at that time, I was so sad for my daughter, and I was so angry at myself that I somehow did not protect her. Angry that I trusted his medical office to take care of my little girl. I was angry and guilt-ridden, and unable to make any plans with lawyers or much of anything else.

The moral of this story is to trust your instincts completely and protect your child *at all costs*. A specialist with pediatrics is always a good choice in these situations, but good and poor medical care can be found everywhere, so be aware.

"Finish each day and done with it. You have done what you could. Some blunders and absurdities no doubt crept in; forget them as soon as you can. Tomorrow is a new day. You shall begin it serenely and with too high a spirit to be encumbered with your old nonsense."

Ralph-Waldo Emerson

27

Listen to Your Heart

I've told you about some of my many experiences with Bri. I've given you some ideas and tips that I've learned along the way. Now, I want to address your needs as the caregiver. As I've mentioned, in the medical mishaps guilt is the first dragon to raise its ferocious head. Guilt for the pregnancy, guilt for the care, guilt for being tired all the time, and guilt for anything and everything involving your child.

Bri was a bit of a surprise pregnancy. I had experienced trouble getting pregnant after the loss of my second pregnancy. So, when Elana, baby two came along, I was elated! She was my miracle baby. Soon after when I found myself pregnant again with Bri, I was shocked! I was still nursing a 15-month-old, so the new pregnancy was definitely not expected. The guilt I felt then centered on getting pregnant by surprise and having to stop nursing baby number two.

After Bri was born, I felt guilt for the time taken away from my barely two-year-old toddler and her having to share her mommy. When Bri was diagnosed, I blamed myself for her autism. I questioned my nutrition during pregnancy, whether or not I had eaten too much fish, or whether there may have been mercury in the water I drank. I wondered whether I had taken enough folic acid or other vitamins. The self-interrogation never ended. I wondered if I'd slept enough due to having two babies at the same time. I pondered whether my body was ready for pregnancy after just having a child a year and a half earlier. I couldn't rest until I knew what went wrong and answered the question of responsibility. Through the years, the guilt would continue and I would look for reasons to blame myself, my husband, or God.

My guilt remained the strongest, most unreasonable, and self- destructive behavior I had for years. Don't do that to yourself. The rate of autism diagnoses is at an all-time high. It is rising in epidemic proportions. You didn't cause it. You can't even fix it, and neither can I.

What we can do, however, is the work necessary to help our babies. Part of that work is in taking care of yourself so that you can be an effective caretaker for your child. The schedule you will be keeping for the next couple of years with a newly diagnosed child will wear out the most highly efficient Olympian. You must keep up! The planning you will have to do for just the immediate future will be exhausting. It will take organization and planning, more than any CEO of any major Fortune 500 Company can handle. You can do it! You won't even realize your strength or determination that you will demonstrate in the upcoming years. I know, I've done it for 18 years and counting as I write this book. I didn't realize what I would be capable of, nor did I know what would have been required of me.

Looking back, I could see part of the picture but not all of it. I was working, teaching, raising three children, trying to maintain my marriage, and desperate to keep my sanity in the midst of a turbulent storm threatening to engulf us all. I know it's exhausting. It can be exhausting for me still on most days, even now. I also know there has been joy and immeasurable perfect love that develops between a caregiver and a child. The amount of time demanded of this job of being a mom or dad, or of any caregiver position for these precious souls, is so worth the work. It is a gift that keeps on giving. In order for you to know this, to truly feel the power and beauty this life can offer, you must be in a good and healthy place yourself. You must find a break and seek it out daily. You must find your spiritual, physical, and emotionally safe place. Sometimes with our schedules, it may seem impossible, but find a few minutes to enjoy your favorite music and blast it as loud as you can. Own it as you take your mind to a quick getaway, and dance a bit, if necessary, while you are unloading the dishwasher, but take that time. Buy a poetry book, and read one a day. Take up knitting. Do you, whatever that may be for you, for the amount of time you have, even if it is five minutes on a given day. I feel like I tried to do that, but I probably did it poorly. Only now, when my other children are grown and independent, and it's mainly Bri and I navigating through the teenage land, do I see that I could have done better for myself and all my kids could have benefitted from a more relaxed mom.

I should have insisted on workout time. I should have used a babysitter more often. I should have listened to my own advice about the village. Let's hope that we are eternal learners, and what we didn't do perfectly the first five months or five years can still be improved upon. Make it a challenge for yourself, that you will take better care of yourself. Make one positive food choice for yourself, and not just eat the leftover toaster pastry that is not even your favorite flavor, but it's all you have time for. Secretly dance to your favorite song like you are the star in your very own show. Enjoy an adult beverage before five, just one. Attend church and sing as loud as you can and receive the necessary blessing on your soul. Listen to your universal message and hear the quiet comforting voice that speaks just for you. Buy a new shirt for yourself, one that doesn't need to be childproof. Matter to yourself, because you matter so very much to your child. You have to be your best. Try every day to give that gift to yourself. While life will give you those difficult days and distractions, remember to get right back on track the next day. Leave the guilt. It serves no purpose. You serve an amazing purpose, but you must take care of yourself first.

"May you live every day of your life."

Jonathan Swift

28

The Truthful Journey

There is a beautiful and famous essay that most people in our world of special education have heard at one time or another. It is titled, "Welcome to Holland", and was written by Emily Perl Kingsley. We thank her for this gifted piece.

Welcome to Holland

I am often asked to describe the experience of raising a child with a disability to try to help people who have not shared that experience to understand it, to imagine how it would feel. It's like this.... When you're going to have a baby, it's like planning a fabulous vacation trip to Italy. You buy a bunch of guidebooks and make your wonderful plans. The Coliseum, the Michelangelo David, the gondolas in Venice. You may learn some handy phrases in Italian. It's all very exciting. After months of eager anticipation, the day finally arrives. You pack your bags and off you go. Several hours later the plane lands. The stewardess comes in and says, "Welcome to Holland". "Holland?!" you say, "What do you mean, Holland?" I signed up for Italy. I am supposed to be in Italy. All my life I've dreamed of going to Italy. But there's been a change in the flight plan. They've landed in Holland there you must stay. The important thing is that they haven't taken you to some horrible, disgusting filthy place full of pestilence, famine, and disease. It's just a different place. So, you must go out and buy a new guidebook. And you must learn a whole new language. And you will meet a whole new group of people you would never have met. It's just a different place.

It's slower paced than Italy, less flashy than Italy. But after you've been there for a while and you can catch your breath, you look around, and you begin to notice that Holland has windmills, Holland has tulips, Holland even has Rembrandts. But everyone you know is busy coming and going from Italy, and they're all bragging about what a wonderful time they had there. For the rest of your life you say, "Yes, that's where I was supposed to go. That's what I planned." The pain of that will never, ever, go away because the loss of that dream is a very significant loss. But if you spend your life mourning the fact that you didn't get to Italy, you may never be free to enjoy the very special, the very lovely things about Holland.

I've heard this essay a million times, but as I add it here, goosebumps are all over my arms. It is a powerful, descriptive way to explain many of our hearts. I had it all planned out for my life. I planned to earn my bachelor's degree in Special Education by age 21, check! I would marry by 22, check! The first baby would arrive after one complete year of marriage, check! Career started and moving in an upwards direction, check! When life started throwing me curveballs, I was steady on my feet for the most part, because all of my plans had worked out nicely for the first decade. Child number two came along, and I was still on my perfectly planned life schedule. Then came along my unexpected trip to Holland, so to speak. I am sure you have your story as well. I have shared pieces of my heart in this book in order for you to know the dreams I had. We all have our dreams. The way I planned my life, I had it all perfectly slated to make my dreams come true. Just like in the beginning when I realized that as a child, I could find a path for myself to help the weaker of us. It was great to find my passion as a young girl. I followed my dreams and made plans for a very helpful career. I am blessed because of it.

I certainly never planned on being a mother of a child with disabilities myself. Although I had my trip to Holland, and it turned out much different than my perfectly planned life, I am here to tell you that my averted trip has been an amazing adventure. Raising my daughter, my very funny, very beautiful, sensory-seeking, limited- verbal angel with autism has been the greatest trip to Holland ever! I would not ask to repeat it though, given the opportunity to have a cure for autism tomorrow, but only for Bri's sake not mine. For her joy and independence, and participation in this very difficult world. For those reasons and more, I would take away her limitations in a minute given the chance. I would joyfully be an unemployed special education teacher if all kids were created equal. Until that miracle comes, I am here to tell you that this is a manageable, wonderful, crazy journey.

When I brought Bri home from the hospital, obviously I had no clue about autism. My pregnancy with her had the obstacles I mentioned before, and I went on with my new infant feeling such gratefulness that she was healthy. I was busy. She was number three, with siblings 2- and 11-years-old, and I had a full busy schedule of teaching, school events, in addition to sports and orchestra for my fourth grader   at that time. All I knew at that time was poor time management, survival cooking, bath and bedtime routines for three, and barely a moment of adult time.

It's funny how you look back at those times and miss them with the whole of your heart. It was exhausting but not traumatic. When I received the whole diagnosis of Bri's disability, it did change our daily routine to include therapy, but for the most part everything kept moving forward. Vacations, family visits, and holidays were planned. Bri fit into all of that the same as her siblings. It was a typical time for all of my kids. Bri participated in everything, even though I'm sure I used every event as a lesson in language acquisition and vocabulary development for her. Still, we were living our lives. As she grew, it was easier some days and more difficult on others. Her frustration level was often challenged by the level of communication she had at that time. She was learning more and wanted to say more, but couldn't always retrieve the words. Behavior, or what looks like behavior, is really just a part of the communication deficit. These deficits frustrated her, resulting in tantrums at times.

Because I was working with the most severe population at the time— autism and behavior—I was not going to let that be the case with Bri if I could help it. I gave her a safe place to express her frustration, but I didn't let her just kick and scream. I scripted it for her. "I know you're mad. Say 'I'm mad!'" "Now, what do you want?" I asked her. I then gave her the carrier phrase again, "I want". She modeled   my words sometimes, but mostly just hesitantly blurt out "Elmo", "cookie", or "drink".

These were the beginning years of learning her language, and my learning how to draw it out of her. It's different when it's your own child, because there's a sense of urgency, one that I didn't feel before in the classroom. Now, I do. My students now, following the Bri era, don't have a chance of me not working as hard as I can on retrieving that early language.

By becoming a parent as well as a teacher of this population, I learned the urgency of helping our kids find their voice. The pace is different now. There's no time to waste, because there's so much more to do. Even though there were milestones of therapy, behavior, and getting bigger and older, the raising of Bri has been, and still is, fun. I find delight in each new skill or verbal expression. The proof that a new therapy worked was a lottery won. The revealed results were immeasurable moments of joy in my life. My work resulted in miracles. I've told you several times to expect the miracles in tiny forms and in huge manifestations. They will occur throughout your child's life. You will appreciate them, and you will see the beauty of Holland. It will look like normal family life somewhat modified at times, which is fine. You are going to experience beauty with your child that is so different from the average because you know how hard both of you worked to get there. Nothing is taken for granted in our lives. You appreciate the new words. The awareness of routine will become apparent over time with your child, and they will develop skills to fit into the family like any other siblings. It may not look exactly the same, but the idea of participation in the household is just as important for your child with special needs, as any of your children.

To raise a child with autism is to be a constant teacher, entertainer, therapist, parent, and friend. This is not an easy role, but it puts you front and center in their lives, so you get to witness the little changes when they come. Every beach trip, every movie, and every shopping trip with Bri was an adventure of some kind where we all learned from each other. I would watch her eating habits on vacation and learn whether or not she was willing to try something new because we were traveling. Sometimes, if she were hungry enough, she did try something new, and it became a milestone. Going to new places like a turtle museum by the beach, and watching her curiosity or listening for new vocabulary even if it was just repeating, became a wonderful addition to our day. These little things that I witnessed on a daily basis make up a lifetime of memories that helped form the individual who is now my daughter. She is still growing and changing, and my experience in Holland has been the adventure of a lifetime. Yours will be, too. The main idea is that this journey you have started, or have been on for a while, is your life. It may not be the trip to Italy you wanted, but a change in flight to Holland. You will survive, and you will thrive. The last 18 years of my life with Bri have been nothing short of a miracle. I have learned more from her than from my graduate degree. I have learned by being her mom, caretaker, therapist, and sometimes her only friend. She has been my friend, as well. She taught me what truly matters. She taught me how words can be funny. To go back and forth with yes, no, yes, no, for what seems an eternity can be wildly entertaining. It can bring the tears of laughter when you see that your child looking right into your eyes and is appreciating the connection you're making with this simple wordplay. You will have many games and many connections with your child that are only yours.

Bri taught me that sometimes you just have to stop and appreciate small moments. We are connected on a level that few people will ever understand or experience. I am solely responsible for her safety, happiness, food, entertainment, and social interactions. I manage her world. I do it with such responsibility and pure joy, hoping the outcome is positive. For the price of being her mother and her guide, she has given me the deepest contentment and respect a person could have for themselves. I know my walk with my daughter is   a gift. She is my muse for a life that we create each day as we see fit. Our relationship is deeper and warmer than most because it is so longstanding. My other two daughters, my beautiful girls of my heart, don't need me like that anymore. They have friends and lives of their own. I could not be prouder of them. They needed me for a time, but unlike Bri, they didn't need me forever. Bri is my small child, in some ways, for an eternity. We often are raising our children through developmental stages at a snail's pace, which translates into time spent on the little things for sometimes months or even years, but eventually it passes unto the next stage.

The kind of patience that we learn to have produces results in a very amazing satisfaction. If it were easy, everyone could do it. You are not everyone. You have a special mission for your life and your child's. It's a good life. When your child is silent for the most part, you play a constant guessing game on what they want or what they are thinking. It becomes a second nature as a young mother, but when this stage lasts the entirety of your baby's childhood, it is something completely different. This doesn't mean that your job and mine is to be completely plugged into the need for them to communicate with us, although that would be best practice. In the real world, you'll be unloading the dishwasher and pressed for time, and need to attend to multiple family members. In these real-life scenarios, you might as well use these opportunities to engage your child into family life and participate with a chore no matter how simple it is. It's a win- win situation. Bri is the only child of mine that smiles when I ask her to put the silverware away. She may be smiling because she's mocking the idea, but nevertheless she smiles and participates.

I engaged her in these tasks at a young age, using therapy language while putting the forks and spoons away, with the request to "Put with same". This is how we speak with the discrete trial therapy, so often our children are familiar with this phrase. Bri would laugh at me, and then do it completely, independent of any more assistance. My theory, in addition to many others, has always been that our children know exactly what is going on. The limitation of language presents as if they don't understand, or that they are young children. In some ways, they are because we keep them that way. We protect and guard them against the dangers of the world, but truthfully, they age like everyone else and are not infinitely children. They are intelligent and capable and must be treated as such.

I believe I have struggled with this idea since Bri's transition from elementary school though her middle- and high-school years. She's still a little girl that needs me in some ways but not always. I'm sure she is bored out of her mind to be with me on some days and not experiencing a more natural teenage experience. There are days that I also need a break from the responsibility as well. However, it's our life, and we don't have a lot of choice in the matter. But I am trying to create a more natural experience for her with helpers that are more age appropriate, and by continuing to transition into a more independent lifestyle for both of us. It will take more planning and work, but it's the right thing to do. It is so difficult to stop treating our children with a disability like they don't have one. The truth is painfully in front of us, but what if they don't know it. What if we can assume competency and intelligence, and reduce the limits that we are putting on them? Making their path develop into a new and more mature age-appropriate experience feels like all the work I did in the early years but next level! This journey has new roads and new paths every step of the way. I am taking on this new level and my new role now. It isn't easy, because my role really hasn't been created yet. Yet, as parents we forage on. We look for new therapies and resources, and we break down more barriers in our schools and in our communities. It is the next step for us and for many of you with kids who are high school age or older on the spectrum.

"We must let go of the life we have planned, so as to accept the one that is waiting for us."

Joseph Campbell

29

Dreams

Dreams come in and out of our sleep, and in and out of our lives. We change our dreams as we go along, compromising because there is no choice but to accept a new dream like in the essay about Holland. As I am writing this book, I am looking forward to a dream that I have dreamt of for over 30 years—a real trip to Italy.

I have traveled once without Bri, out of the country to a family wedding in Israel. It was an amazing and glorious trip where I learned to breathe again. I took time for myself. It was wonderful. I had my middle daughter with me, so it was still a family adventure. Bri survived and had a wonderful time with grandmother and another sister back home. I waited all those years to travel. We planned our long-awaited trip to Italy, my dream destination, a honeymoon with my husband, 30-some years later than it should have been. We had always found reasons why we couldn't take a trip like this. There were new jobs, a new mortgage, and eventually children to raise, which delayed the dream.

It took months of planning for a week of fun, but it was all worth it. The planning alone of what I might wear, what I would see, and what I could bring back with me were all a part of this initial planning. The point is, you don't have to stop being you, or being a couple, or simply having a little bit of an adult life. It might be delayed for 30 years, which is a pretty long time, but hopefully this information I've provided will help you to plan earlier and better than I did. At the core is the fear of letting go of the control of our children and their lives—the nagging thought that only you can do this job. We somehow think that the world will fall apart if we're not the exact person to take care of all the details. I am learning that we must let go of this fear for our own sanity, and for the welfare of our children. Family, friends, and trusted caregivers in our lives can help and probably want to from time to time.

I became very emotional as I wrote these words because it's the fear that I have been hanging on to for so long. Actually, it was easier to do stuff myself rather than to ask for help most of the time. The planning, the arranging, the extra costs, and the worry made it easier to detour the idea of any personal life. It's the same for teachers. We would rather go to work on our deathbed than write lesson plans for a substitute. In just seems more difficult to explain in writing what we have been doing, breathing, and executing for the children. Still, it must be done. You will be more of a parent if you have a tiny piece of this life for yourself every once in a while. You still will be a good parent, and your child will still adore you. You will be a calmer, better version of yourself when you take some time for yourself, especially for a special trip or something that is just for you. I hope you plan many little getaway weekends for yourself, as well as fun family trips. I hope you don't wait as long as I waited. Live a full life, it is possible even with a child with special needs.

Italy

The trip of a lifetime, a dream that was born before even my children, is coming true. It's really going to happen. Our family is on alert to watch Bri. My mother has flown in and arrived, so I begin to give her directions, our safety concerns, and an inventory of the food in the house. Of course, the refrigerator is stocked with a month's supply of frozen waffles, turkey bacon, and even the forbidden soda. The pantry is filled with cereal, chips, and toaster pastries. I 've cleaned Bri's room and organized all of her beads, coloring supplies, and stuffed animals. I've charged the tablets, mp3 players, lined up the headphones, and looked around to see what else I could possibly do to make this work. For weeks, I explained to Bri, mommy and daddy are going on an airplane and we will be back soon. I told her that her grandma is coming and her sister will be around to visit with her while I am gone. I've made a calendar with pictures of us and an airplane for each day we will be gone, and I've circled the day we will return. I tell her every morning and every night how much I love her, and how I will bring her back a present from Italy. My guilt has appeared, and I've desperately tried to shut it down.

I need this trip! My marriage needs this trip. My heart has been aching for a fantasy trip like this my whole life. I deserve it. I will be better at all my roles when I return from this dream vacation.   I desperately try to convince myself, but the guilt, the monstrous guilt, is always looming in the back of my mind. We finally arrive in Italy. It is more beautiful than all my dreams. It is breathtaking. The experience of getting on the plane from Atlanta to New York, then onto Milan, was fun and adventurous.

Slowly, my husband and I begin talking to each other again, not about the kids, life, and bills, but about this beauty in front of us. We take in the sights. We spend hours on a train, after the night spent on the plane, simply to just sit and watch. Just us on the train for hours to Rome is magnificent. From little towns, walls of graffiti, countryside landscapes to the snow-capped Alps, our view is breathtaking.
I decide what to eat, where to sit, whatever choices necessary, just for myself. This time alone was needed,

and I've enjoyed every second of it. For the first few hours, I decide to shop for gifts for all of my children, probably to put aside the guilt of my indulgence. Still, I enjoy every part of the trip. We eat pasta. We eat unbelievably fresh delicious food and gelato several times a day. We sit in cafes and take our time. We even argue a little bit, due to the tension of waiting so long to do this and for all of these years that weighed on us both.

The floral markets, the sculptures, and the Vatican are our only focus afterward. Breakfast is a fantasy. We walk into a red velvet- draped theatre with tall glass vases filled with the most beautiful purple and white flowers. Tables are filled with salmon, prosciutto, tiny little turkey links, eggs the color of the sun, cheeses from all around the region, and hot fresh rolls. The coffee served at our table is the most elegant that I have ever tasted, along with another carafe of hot steamed milk poured into the prettiest china from somewhere back in time. Champagne is also part of breakfast, with every kind of freshly squeezed juice that you could imagine, along with every condiment needed like honey, jams, nuts, and chocolates. Such beauty, such luxury, a trip of a lifetime, and so healing in so many ways. Yes, it is deserved.

Now, I am the kind of person who can see beauty in everything on an average day, but this trip was so special. I took my time in the shower. I dressed in fashionable clothes, accessorized, played with my makeup, and debated on shoe selections. My focus was all about me and this trip, and it didn't take too long to get used to the luxury.

The balance I am always reaching for was met during this short little week. I was definitely better for it when we returned home. It took me no less than 17 years of my daughter's life to take this trip. It probably wasn't necessary, but it was for me. When we went, I was ready, and I believe Bri was as well. Grandma took perfect care of her. She had a great time. I'm not even sure of what time means   to our kids. I am also not sure if she was aware of how long a week was, but she had a mini vacation without mom. I should have done that years before I did. My point, of course, is that on this journey of raising a child with a disability of any kind, or any children, it's important to take care of yourself, and that other family members as well as you, do for your child. Balance is the most important, in nature and in our lives, in order to be able to achieve the best outcome consistently for all of your loved ones, including yourself.

I had my dream vacation, my breath of fresh air, and time to heal and think. It was lovely and left me with the best memories for a lifetime. I look forward to planning our next trip. I have given you the paraphrased version of this break from my reality, but I do not mean to elude that it was easy. The idea was one thing, but making it come true took so much discussion, planning, and second thoughts. I owe a special thanks to my principal for allowing me to take the time in the middle of February during the school year. This trip was so necessary for my family. I am sure there will be more than once where time off will benefit yours as well, and you must feel good about all of your decisions. You'll need to evaluate what timing works best for you. For me, there was never the time when she was little. I allowed my guilt or overprotection, or just plain being a mom, take over any ideas of a getaway with my husband or even to plan a girl's trip. I may have waited too long to figure that out, so that's why I hope that your timing in taking care of yourself will open up to you earlier than it did for me.

As I write these last chapters, I am looking in the very near future of my daughter, her turning 18 and all that encompasses with that milestone. I've started gathering pictures of her childhood to decorate for the party, and it has sent me down a nostalgic journey for days. There was so much I may have done correctly, but looking back from a different place always makes you aware of how much you have learned along the way, and sometimes you wish you could do things over. Don't do that to yourself. On the other hand, as I look at the many smiling moments of her precious face, and it makes me realize that she has well taken care of and happy. I also understand that as I learned more, I did more, and hopefully, I'll do it better going forward. At this stage of her life, I am making every effort to give her the dignity of being a young lady and not a child. It is difficult, as she's a person who still demonstrated an equal love for Elmo and Elton John, but this is who she is. She is not my baby anymore, and I am teaching myself how to speak to her and treat her like the 18-year- old young lady that she has become. The future projects that I have facing me, like getting her ready for the next adult stages in her life, are daunting.

I have become an expert, so to speak, of babies through age 18, and of children with disabilities, especially autism, but I guarantee you that I am still learning every day. I have a student who will make shapes and now numbers out of any minute piece of material he can get his hands on. His last artistry was made out of jelly from a cereal bar, with which he used to carefully create the number nine. In the past in my classroom, I may have wiped it away and redirected him to more appropriate writing materials. Now, I question that teaching. If his little soul is thinking about number nine so much that he must make it out of jelly, I let him. His brain is telling him that there is nothing more important than numbers right now, and it must be made. This is the artistic beauty and mystery of autism. In these situations, especially as teachers, we must really think about what is being processed in their heads and wonder if the battle is worth it. I will, of course, eventually wipe down the table from his crumbs and give him paper and a marker, or clay with templates to make his number nine. But at that moment, I don't have to burst his bubble. This example illustrates that autism is one complex disorder that enables a beautiful child to demonstrate intelligence in many novel ways. The creative level alone that our children show us every day with the way they play, shows us how they are thinking. We must become the most skilled observers of behavior to see it all.

He's the child who takes the tiny red frog manipulatives and instead of counting to five and following the direction of the teacher, decides to form a number five with all of the frogs. Pure genius is demonstrated, but it's definitely out of the box. He is still demonstrating what he knows. He showed me that he knew his numbers, but showed me with jelly or frogs. Maybe it's time to look at that as the incredible expression of knowledge that it is, and to stop trying to correct it to fit into our traditional ways of learning.

"Life is a book and there are a thousand pages I have not yet read." Cassandra Clare

Summary

In the beginning, I wanted to be a special education teacher who would make a difference in the lives of children. I wanted to help parents by loving their children and teaching them the best way I had learned in college. A lightning strike later, and I am the parent of a child with a disability myself. My story is not unique, even with colleagues in my field who have also been gifted with special children.

My story is only unique in that I humbly accept that this child of mine has made me a better person than I ever would have been without her in my life. She has taught me patience and tested it! She has shown me how exciting it is to see the moon for the first time. She has helped me to understand that every day is a new day for learning. I have experienced highs and lows with her for 18 years, beginning with the answered prayer that I prayed for her only be born healthy and not to have needed the open-heart surgery that the doctor had advised of with that first ultrasound early in my pregnancy.

She and I have survived life, and we have done it together with a bit of mess and a lot of laughter. Raising a child to adulthood usually becomes somewhat easier as they grow and show independence.

They grow into teenagers and want you around less and less. Bri and I spent many more years at Chucky Cheese than any parent should have to endure, along with the continuation of Elmo birthday parties for decades, which evolved into her joining my friends for Mexican food on a Friday. Whatever it is, we have done it together. We still do it together. I have learned from this Earth angel that our work is never done. What we learned yesterday will not be enough for tomorrow, and the question of what comes next is forever our motto.

I have learned from being her mom that I am not Superwoman, and it's okay.

I love her so much and my other children. I want to take care of all of them sometimes, but I am tired. There are times when I want off of the autism train. I don't want to plan everything, every day. It's during those times that I give myself permission to take a break if possible.

In addition, my children have also learned from each other. They are the best sisters to Bri. They are strong and protective about autism awareness and have been their whole lives.

My oldest daughter is a nurse working with children with autism. My second daughter is studying in the field of medicine and participating in an internship with young children with autism. Bri has influenced all of us. Not to be so Pollyanna, as my father used to say, it's not an easy path. Everyone has a different view of their personal destiny with a child with a disability. For me, and my family, Bri is a source of light and growth. I am eternally grateful to have her as my daughter. I'm also grateful for my career of over 30 years now, where I have learned from each and every precious student who has ever walked through my classroom. For the families that I've met who shared similar stories like mine, who provided camaraderie, and to the families that my experiences helped to guide some of their next steps with their young children, for all of these experiences, I am changed. I am grateful for all the lessons learned.

I will continue to grow and learn as much about autism as I can, and together we will have more solutions than problems. It is a trip down a yellow brick road for sure, but you are not alone. Take it one day at a time. When you don't have an answer, find someone to help you find it. Resources are available, and the world is becoming more intelligent and tolerant to help make a better place for our children to grow in. Each child with autism or any disability is different. The one truth I know is that each child has something to teach us. Each child has a personality and a beautiful soul, and it is our job to discover who they are. It is our privilege to teach them how to best navigate their individual journey. Enjoy the process, take pleasure in the small steps, and take care of the whole family, including yourself.

"We are each of us angels with only one wing, and we can fly by embracing one another."

Luciano De-Crescenzo

Epilogue

New therapies are on the horizon. I have witnessed myself progress that can only be referred to as a miracle. I recently met up with a student who I taught as a little boy through middle school. At that time, his language was limited to requesting and answering basic questions. He currently has started a new therapy along the lines of the Rapid Prompting Method. This involves using a letter board to spell based on lessons that are age appropriate in subject matter, and questions are asked about what is read to the student. They begin by answering with spelling. The philosophy behind this method is to assume competence in these individuals with autism.

In front of my eyes, without prompting from a therapist except to hold the letter board, he spelled out to me letter by letter. He spoke to me through his letters, as if he had been speaking his whole life. This is new information for me at this time, but I have enrolled Bri into the same therapy. The name for this therapy is called Spelling to Communicate. We may be on the cusp of a new way for our children to reach us. Not all children respond to all therapies equally, but as I mentioned in the book, try everything.

I would my readers to stay abreast of all new information. Research it all for the benefit of your child. Never stop fighting for them. Never lose hope. We love our children and support them as they are, but at the same time we must keep searching and trying new therapies and strategies to give them the best opportunity to learn and to communicate with us.

About the Author

Lynn Shebat is a special education teacher, specializing in autism and behavior disorders. She has taught in Florida, North Carolina, South Carolina and Georgia. She is a teacher with decades of experience at various grade level.

Lynn holds a M.S. Degree in Special Education from Georgia State University,
and completed her undergraduate degree at Florida International University.

Lynn was nominated for Teacher of the Year for 2018, for her current school. She has been teaching special needs preschool for the last seven years, and has served as the department chair, and behavioral coach for the Positive Behavior Intervention team. She has worked with the most severe populations for much of her career. Lynn enjoys the challenge of learning about each child's interests, strengths and weaknesses.

She is honored to publish her first book with 1010 Publishing. She lives in Atlanta, Georgia with her husband, three daughters, and a son-in-law.

Made in the USA
Columbia, SC
17 July 2019